FIRE & CLAY

BOOK ONE

KAARONICA TÆFÉ EVANS-WARE

SASHAKIRA™
CREATIONS
ANN ARBOR, MICHIGAN

This book is a work of fiction. Although some characters, incidents, and period details are based upon historical documents or are used fictitiously, the work in general is a product of the author's imagination.

Original title: Fire & Clay: Book One
Third Edition: December 2013
Published by Sashakira Creations.
kaaronicaevansware.wordpress.com

The logo of Sashakira Creations is a design of Kaaronica Evans-Ware. Cover art by Kaaronica Evans-Ware. Photograph copyright is licensed through Shutterstock Images. Hand-drawn map by Rudolph Ware, III.

Publisher's Cataloging-in-Publication data
Evans-Ware, Kaaronica Tæfé.
Fire & Clay: Book One/Kaaronica Tæfé Evans-Ware.

p. cm.

1. Senegal—History – Islam – Slavery, 1700's – Fiction. 2. Jinn—Human and Jinn Marriages—Polygamy. 3. Spirit Spouses 4. Futa—Senegal River—Slave Raids. 5. Historical fiction. 6. Speculative fiction. 7. Paranormal fiction. 8. Islamic fiction. 9. Romance fiction.

ISBN: 978-0615813882

Printed in the United States of America.

For my descendants:
May you always seek protection, truth and
wisdom.

ACKNOWLEDGEMENTS

I would like to thank my mother and father, Judith and Andrew, for passing their love of reading and writing on to me.

Thank you Butch, my brilliant husband, for sparking my imagination once again. I am so grateful for the hundreds of deeply spiritual conversations about this fictional world. You get it and I'm so very glad you do!

To my siblings, Andrew, Kyra, and Kofi, you are the best inspiration. I would also like to thank my eldest child Samonia for reading my first draft and offering important suggestions and comments. Shamarra for coming to my rescue as I finished the last chapters. Ismai'ilia, Rabi'a, and Idris for providing the necessary comedic break at the right times. I want to thank the first storyteller I ever heard, my Aunt Vivienne, for sharing family lore. Lawana "Elle" Holland-Moore, thank you once again for lighting the fire!

And last but not least, I would like to thank the incomparable Cheikhouna Lo for his immense wisdom and guidance on this project. Babacar Fall, for his enthusiastic support over the years.

TABLE OF CONTENTS

Map

FIRE & CLAY

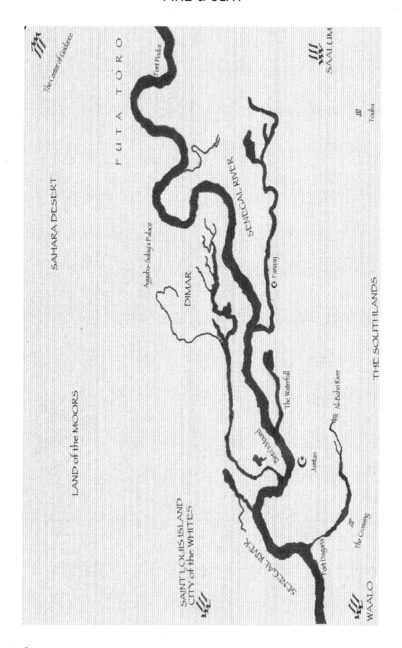

"God is never surprised."

Chapter One

THE IRON DOME

The man and the woman trembled uncontrollably. Their armpits were moist with sweat. Their hearts, which they hadn't thought about until now, beat wildly in their chests. Hiding in the tall grass, not far from their feet was the thing that had tricked them.

The hatred in the thing's heart had begun to grow a very long time ago, when he first heard the chatter about the new creature and all that had gone into making it. He had gone to the great gates where the figure was propped outside. He had wanted to ignore it—to pretend that it was only a passing fancy soon to be discarded.

But he was curious. At first glance he could see that it was too ornate to be easily abandoned. Even sitting lifeless it was unlike anything he had seen before. He lifted stones high in the air and propelled them at the figure. They made a hollow clanking sound, still the figure did not move. The clanking sound perplexed him. What was this thing made of? He flew inside its gaping mouth and out through its anus. It was dark and seemed empty. "Whatever this thing is, surely it is not nobler than me!" he thought.

He flew in and out of it several times more to be sure. He raised the form in the air and threw it. When it fell, he struck it. Still it did not move. As he hovered over the empty shell of man, the thing swore that if he was to rule over it he would kill it and if it were to rule over him he would rebel. Thus began the longest war known to man.

September 17, 2010 Touba, Senegal
Eighth Day of Shawwal, 1431 AH

Not far from the holy city of Touba stood a boxy, clay-colored prison. Desert sand, that relentless intruder, began to blanket the stone floors the day the prison was abandoned by humans hundreds of years before. It was now completely overrun. The contours of its walls and floors were almost hidden from the eyes of men. Its unkempt terrace was now a home only to palmettos, mice, and lizards. When men walked far away enough from their beaten paths to happen upon this structure—and few ever did— only its broken roof would distinguish it from the other mounds of earth and sand. Few men had stayed long enough to explore its crumbling ancient cells and dungeons, or to finger the rusted hinges that had once held heavy iron gates in place. It was not now, nor had it ever been, the kind of place where a man felt comfortable spending time.

Not every place that looks empty really is. For many, many years, Zamar had waited for her shift at the prison to begin by flying to the rooftop terrace to be alone with her thoughts. She was a guard and interrogator. She was terrible at both jobs. But she stayed employed thanks to her marriage to the warden, Jaag. The job suited her ill, but

Jaag did what he could to make it easier for her nature to accept. He protected her from the most ferocious prisoners. He made sure she never saw how the other guards pummeled the violent ones into submission. When they were prayerful prisoners, he allowed her to pray with those whom she guarded. Her fellow guards followed Jaag's edict to the letter and kept some things hidden from her. Some things she was aware of, but did not really care to know. Of other things she was truly ignorant. For a long time, the iron-walled dome hidden underground on the prison's west side had been one of those things. Only an unmarked and unremarkable three-foot crevice in the earth opened the way to it. And ever since its purpose had been revealed to her she had spent a great deal of time there. Today, the iron dome would receive a visitor that would change the course of Zamar's life forever.

It all started just after dawn with commotion at the outskirts of Touba, miles away. Zamar had been watching the edge of town from her rooftop perch since well before dawn, when the loudspeakers jolted men from their slumber with the call to prayer. All of the faithful were called, but it was mostly mothers and maids who answered. They rose to pray and prepare breakfast while their men slept and their houses were still.

What caught and kept Zamar's eye was the sight of two little boys who had been begging for alms since she finished her morning prayer just after first light. They went from door to door, assembling a breakfast from the neighborhood's dinner leftovers. They laughed and they argued; they pushed and they shoved. A very homely three-legged dog followed them everywhere. The boys shouted stern warnings at the mutt and subjected it to occasional half-hearted stonings. Still, they gave it occasional scraps from their coffee cans, so they must have known that it would not abandon them.

Zamar marveled greatly at humans. She could admit to herself that she liked their smiles, especially those of children, and her traveling breakfast party was now rejoicing. Moments after sunrise, a light-brown skinned woman had wiped the sleep from her eyes and smiled at the boys at her door, before bringing them a plastic bag full of frozen bissap juice. Instinctively, they retreated to a safe place with this precious haul, moving just beyond the town's limits and sitting at the foot of a baobab tree that shielded them from the sun rising over the town. They laughed and drank the juice. It was red, and cold, and sweet. The dog, however, had not followed them into the shade of the tree, he stood at the edge of the street that marked the confines of the city, ears raised, and growled.

The boys could not see it, but an awful procession marched just before their eyes. Zamar did not see as well as she once had, but even across the miles she could see clearly what was hidden to them. She could make out four airy forms—bounty hunters she was sure. Their long red and white robes signaled their purpose to those who could see them. They staggered alongside a chariot that transported an agitated beast. If the children had looked directly to their left in just the right light, they may have momentarily glimpsed the shimmering outline of the beast, like waves of heat rising from the desert floor. They would have seen a freakishly gaunt figure pulling frantically to free itself from some imperceptible bonds.

Zamar witnessed the scene in its fullness. As the beast freed its hand, two of the vigilant bounty hunters pounced on him and hammered him with fists that moved faster than a mere human could have seen in any light. The being shook off the punches and spat at its captors, trying to pierce their robes and skins. The four bounty hunters restrained and muzzled the prisoner with their subtle cords. They stabilized their wobbling chariot and the unearthly steed that drew it, and continued on.

The boys were just finishing their bissap. They threw the empty baggy almost directly at the feet of the bounty hunter that brought up the rear of the procession without ever seeing him. They made their way back across the city limits into Touba, and the traveling prison continued to trace its path just outside of the town's hallowed ground, where they were forbidden ever to tread.

☪

Zamar knew the captive. His form was familiar and unfamiliar at once, yet the scent that came to her over the wind was unmistakable. It was ancient and awful. The beast bound to the cart was Nemacus. To make sure her old eyes saw correctly she concealed herself and flew down to the cart. The prisoner was indeed missing his right hand. As she got closer she could smell faint traces of human waste and blood clinging to his ethereal form and mingling with his own peculiar stench. *Where on Earth did they find him? What in God's name was he doing when they did?*

Nemacus was no longer the hulking leader of a vicious army. His robust build, square shoulders and regal airs were either gone or perfectly concealed. What Zamar saw now was a withered and broken jinn.

Still, seeing him emaciated and demoralized disturbed her. For hundreds of years, her mind had devised countless ways to take her revenge on him. She fervently hoped that God would give her vengeance in this life and not make her wait until the next. Seeing him in this condition both satisfied and disappointed her. He must have suffered much, but not nearly enough. Zamar glowered at Nemacus, thinking: what am I to do with this shell of a jinn? How can I make him pay for what he did to me and my family now?

She was determined to get something from him—an explanation at least—even if it meant nursing him back to health just to break him.

"I was just wearing those men! I didn't kill them!" Nemacus yelled at Ben Al-Hajji, the largest of the bounty hunters. He did not respond right away, he merely wrapped extra chains around his prisoner and pulled them until they squeezed him tightly. Then he spoke: "If I were you I wouldn't say another word."

The bounty hunters dragged Nemacus off the street and into the halls of the prison, where a lone guard greeted them with a languid expression. "What have you half-breeds brought us today?" he asked, smirking slightly. The door guard was far shorter than his visitors, a stubby jinn with thick wiry bristles covering his arms, legs, and chest. The airy robes that hid his form barely concealed the powerful frame beneath.

"Watch it!" Shouted Ben Al-Hajji. A patient creature by nature, the leader of the band of bounty hunters was now on edge. The struggle to restrain Nemacus had withered his calm temperament.

"What? You don't like me pointing out your human blood? Or is it your jinn blood you have issue with?" The stocky guard stared into the bounty hunter's face with a menacing expression. He took one long step toward the bounty hunter to close the gap between them and to illustrate fearlessness.

"Neither!" replied Ben Al-Hajji. He too bridged the gap between them by taking a step towards the door guard. "We are proud to have a foot in each world. We just don't like the jealousy."

The guard scoffed at the suggestion. *Jealous of what? But why bother arguing with half-breeds about genealogy?* he thought. So instead he asked about the chained jinn they were escorting. "And, this one here, is he an elemental too?"

"No!" Nemacus tried to exclaim, "I'm a pure breed like you!" As soon as he spoke the four hunters battered his body with frightening speed, their hands growing in size and changing shape to resemble large clubs. Nemacus appeared to lose consciousness. His eyes closed and his ethereal form went completely limp.

"Enough talk!" said one of the bounty hunters. "Yes," continued Ben Al-Hajji, "we have other business. Do we leave him here?"

"No, bring him inside," the door guard said, opening the gate.

The bounty hunters dragged Nemacus further inside. "You're going to want to put him in a cell right away," said Ben Al-Hajji.

Looking carefully at Nemacus for the first time, the door guard asked, "And why's that?"

"Don't let his weakened appearance fool you," Ben Al-Hajj replied. "He's frightfully strong."

The door guard strained to look through Nemacus' form and see his fundamental nature—his flame. It seemed to flicker feebly. Using this kind of sight—ordinary for jinn, and even for many hybrids, but beyond the capacity of all except the most gifted humans—the door guard took the measure of Nemacus: "Are you trying to convince me that this decrepit jinn can cause harm?"

The bounty hunters scoffed before sharing a sad furtive glance. Ben Al-Hajji broke their silence. "I don't know what *you* see when you look at him, but he is far from weak. He killed one of my men. That is not an easy task."

The door guard walked in front of them, guiding the way. "What's so surprising about that?" He said with an air of disdain. He stopped walking to face them before continuing. "That comes with your profession. It's a natural risk of your job."

Ben Al-Hajji was now getting irritated. "You should have more respect for those who give their lives doing their jobs. Especially jobs you couldn't do and wouldn't have the courage to do even if God gave you the ability."

He still held tightly onto his quarter of Nemacus, a task easier to manage now that Nemacus was exhausted. "We 'half-breeds,' as you affectionately call us, are specially suited to cross between the worlds to capture rogue jinn. Even a fool like you must know this! What you seem *not* to know is that some of them are so ferocious and deadly that sometimes one of us must knowingly sacrifice his own life to keep the team from being slaughtered. Half-breed lives may be cheap to you, but I served with Farah for ages. Of course, *you* wouldn't know anything about that. You have a meaningless job that serves only you. You just stand by that door looking stupid every single day of your miserable…"

"That will be quite enough from the two of you," said a voice that sounded like footsteps on gravel.

☪

Everyone turned about to see the warden, Jaag, gliding in from outside. He was an intimidating jinn. His natural form was something like the shape of a man, but with shoulders that were impossibly wide. If a thing of flesh were to have shoulders so broad set upon such narrow hips and legs it would topple over. Jaag's oblong head was also large and imposing with small, wide-set eyes. Course white hair covered part of his head. But not the brow, chin, and top, as it might have on a man. Instead it sprouted at the height of his eyes and sat in a stiff even mane covering the top half of his head. His hairline, as it were, started in the middle of his long face. The few times that humans had seen him as he was, they screamed in terror and ran. A long time ago, a man had seen him emerging from a river and the man's heart stopped. Even for the jinn, he was a shock to the eyes.

He spoke again, slowly, like low raspy footfalls: "Take the prisoner directly to the iron dome."

"But, warden, you said prisoners go to the interrogation room first," the door guard said.

"Yes. And I also said that if a prisoner with a history of violence comes to us in an agitated state they are to be taken where?" Jaag asked.

"To the iron dome," said the guard, bowing his head in shame for being reprimanded in front of the lowly bounty hunters.

"This," Jaag began, "is Nemacus. Had you not slept through so many meetings, you would know of him." He paused, raising a long sharp finger at the stubby guard. "You would know that even in our chains he could twirl into a powerful whirlwind at any moment. He could easily shatter the walls around him, destroying this prison, and killing all save the most resilient of jinn. These so-called half-breeds that you deride are the only reason you are still alive."

The door guard, looked up briefly and saw that Jaag was still glaring at him, so he cast his eyes downward again.

"If not for the special abilities of our elemental friends here," Jaag bowed with genuine respect toward Ben Al-Hajji, "he would have extinguished your fire the moment he saw you."

The lead bounty hunter lowered his head, returning the gesture.

At this Warden Jaag spoke again, "We are sorry for your loss." Then he turned and began gliding down the corridor toward the dome, with the stocky guard sliding alongside him.

Ben Al-Hajji and his men looked again at one another and began pulling Nemacus toward the iron dome.

Jaag looked around. "Where is Zamar?" he whispered to the guard, sure that the hunters would not hear. They had not. Even so, the limp figure of Nemacus seemed to twitch at the sound of her name.

"She is late again warden," the guard sighed quietly in response.

"Ben Al-Hajji, good fortune has found you!" Jaag said gliding quickly down the corridor to the bounty hunters. "You and your men are about to get a guided tour of our infamous iron dome."

"Ha!" chuckled the bounty hunter. The truth is that you 'pure-breeds' cannot enter that dome without getting stuck in it yourselves! You need us and this will cost you." The bounty hunters dragged the broken jinn down the corridor, following Jaag and the guard to the iron dome.

☪

Once or twice every thousand years a pure-bred jinn is born that can pass through iron. The rest hate it intensely. Just to be touched directly by iron—or by salt—causes them tremendous pain. More than this, however, iron is reviled for its capacity to bind them. Jaag, foreboding though he was, stopped well short of the dome and allowed the hunters and their prey to pass. Even the half-breed bounty hunters braced themselves as they pushed Nemacus into the cell. For a moment, they feared that their prisoner was that once-in-a-lifetime jinn immune to its iron walls, for after they pushed him into the cell and closed its iron door, he howled and whirled instead of instantly freezing. Just as the warden had feared, the mighty Nemacus tried to twirl his body and swell in size, as he stepped toward the door.

He did not make it even a step. First his feet, then his legs and abdomen changed from translucent fire into something resembling solid rock. As Jaag, the guards, and the hunter peered through the small blurry crystal into the dome, they saw the most hunted jinn of a generation became a contorted, wild-eyed statue.

"Argh! Let me out of here!" Nemacus groaned. Now, and until death or release, only his eyes and mouth would function.

"Why was he still able to move?" asked the stubby guard.

"I do not know. I have never seen it before," Jaag replied. "He may not be immune to iron, but he is powerful. All of the others were hardened instantaneously."

"I can assure you," said Ben Al-Hajji, "he is not like the others. It is not for nothing that he was wanted in thirteen lands on three continents."

At this, the three other bounty hunters glanced at their chief. Ben Al-Hajji understood immediately, and spoke again. "Warden Jaag, we should go now. We know that unlike some, you honor the old ways. In the time of our fathers no exchange like this took place without a proper feast, and we saw the mounds of carrion just beyond the prison walls. We ask your permission to collect our reward now and depart without feasting on the flesh of beasts together. Like you, we love custom, but those who wanted Nemacus for themselves will come after us and we must take flight."

"Of course," replied the warden. "You have earned your reward and you shall have it," he said, motioning toward the guard. "Can I not persuade you to feast with us?"

"Any day but today," Ben Al-Hajji said, "the risk is too great. The backlash will be severe. Did you know that the Americans offered 40 brides with their reward? You should beware. Someone will come for him, the price is too great."

"I am fully prepared for that eventuality," said Jaag, nodding. He paused for a moment and then laughed. "40 Brides eh? You should have taken Nemacus to them!"

"Loyalty is better than lust old friend."

"Is it now?" Jaag chuckled. "At the risk of sounding like my ignorant door guard, I think that may be your human side talking."

"Possibly. However, truth is truth." Ben Al-Hajji continued, "Loyalty is all we have in this world. If you really want to know why I brought him here, if you really want to know what loyalty has to do with it, you need only ask your wife, Zamar."

"Ah Zamar! That jinniyya of mine is full of secrets!" exclaimed the warden.

"She is also very late for work..." muttered the stubby guard who had just returned carrying four large white muslin pouches laden with jewels, gold, lamps, and scrolls.

Before the words had left his lipless mouth, Jaag's long hand extended with his fingers wrapping around the guard's throat nearly ripping it from his shoulders. "Do not speak!" My wife is none of your business. This elemental is a friend to Zamar and to me; you are a friend to no one. Shut up, give them their reward, and remember your place."

The guard did not speak; he merely nodded and complied with his order, handing the large sacks to the crew of bounty hunters.

"Ben Al-Hajji," Jaag continued, turning towards the bounty hunter. "I divided Farah's share among you. I then doubled all of the shares." The three other hunters began to smile widely; their leader only nodded. "I trust you will find your loyalty well-placed, even if others have promised wives?"

"I do indeed, my friend!" exclaimed the tall half-breed.

"Then go in peace. I shall discuss this matter of loyalty with my own bride, as you have suggested." With this the bounty hunters flew through the winding corridor that led back from the dome, carrying their fortune in tow.

They bent their forms effortlessly to pass back through the narrow three-foot crevice that concealed the subterranean dome and its anterooms. As they emerged, they saw the sun was still only slowly climbing toward its zenith. Their unearthly steed was just inside one of the crumbling clay walls, hidden from the sight of men. As usual there were no men around. They cloaked their treasure—just in case—and loaded it onto their cart.

☪

"Warden," whispered the stumpy guard, "may I speak?"

"Yes, Sangoot, you may," answered Jaag.

"Do you really believe the Americans offered brides?"

Jaag motioned him back toward his post as he responded, "Yes, I most certainly do. Across the ocean, few of the children of Adam know that we exist. The jinn in that land can get away with just about anything."

"Well," Sangoot continued, "why did the Americans want him so badly?"

"From what I hear he was long wanted for many crimes," began Jaag. "A small yet powerful band of jinn from our clan, lieutenants of Samra'zin the Just, crossed the water to capture him; this must have been sixty years ago. They wanted the price on his head and to bring him to justice, but after the fight to subdue him, they dared not try to bring him back. They imprisoned him in an abandoned well. The children of Adam had dug that well two hundred years ago, hoping to settle there. Instead, they found the water very brackish so they abandoned it. There were no streams nearby, so no one settled in the area. Soon wild grasses covered the land and hid the well. No one disturbed it for a long time. It should have made an excellent prison."

"It didn't?" Sangoot queried.

"The prison held him fine. The salty water would not have been enough to restrain Nemacus, but the well was cut through a salt deposit, so its walls alone pained him greatly, and he could not fly. Samra'zin's men wisely feared that this would not be enough. They had half-breeds wrap him with a heavy iron chain, they fixed the chain to a rock, and they hung him upside down in the well."

"There is no god but God!" exclaimed Sangoot. "Forget the escape, how did he survive?"

"Ben Al-Hajji tried to tell you; he is not like others," explained Jaag. "He did not fight the chains. He did not try to scrape away at the salt walls. He did not wail at the pain. He lowered his flame and waited. For twenty years our people left a guard at the mouth of the well. After a time, they grew lax in their watch, and confident that their prison was inescapable. They left and went on to pursue the business of jinn. One year passed before they returned to check on him."

Sangoot interrupted, "And he was gone?"

"Of course he was. After a frantic search they learned that he had been living with a human woman, a widow, who had settled on the land near the well. Soon after she arrived, she began dreaming of a beautiful man trapped inside a well. The dream came to her night after night. Day after day, she went out in search of this beautiful man. After a time, she found the well. He called out to her with a deep manly voice. The woman ran home and returned with a ladder that she lowered down into the well. He called up to her again, telling her he could not climb the ladder because he was chained. She ran back home, returned with an axe, and climbed down into the well."

"She did all of this without once asking who put him in the well or why they chained him!" Sangoot marveled.

"In the darkness of the well," Jaag patiently recounted, "she could not see him as he was, trapped in his jinn form. She hacked away at the lock on his chain and it unraveled. He fell into the water at the bottom of the well, but its salt was not enough to keep him from changing form. When they climbed into the moonlight, he was in the form of the very handsome man from her dreams. It was a man he had once briefly worn for sport, so he knew it well and could borrow its likeness."

"Nemacus lived with her and shared her bed. She had his children but did not know. She could not see them. Children like that—like the bounty hunters—may have feet in both worlds, but can only exist in one." Jaag was silent for a moment, as if reflecting on something. "They follow the state of their fathers. You know how it goes."

"All too well," the stumpy jinn said, feeling bad about the things he said.

"You would do well to speak better to those like Ben Al-Hajji," Jaag said, chiding his subordinate. "Their way is not easy. Most die very young. Sometimes they know their mothers, but their mothers almost never know them. Those women think they are barren."

"Of course," Sangoot affirmed, "How could they think otherwise?

"Exactly," the warden continued, "their bellies do not swell; they cannot see their own children; they pass clots of blood and believe they are fruitless."

Jaag paused for a moment. "I suppose in a sense they are. The seed of fire burns their wombs. If they lay with us, they can no longer bear children of clay. Anyway, by the time the jinn in America realized what had happened, the woman had gone mad. She did not know it, but she had twelve spirit children living in the forest around her and Nemacus had moved on to his next conquest."

"Why do you suppose he fathers so many half-jinn children? It almost seems like he's collecting them," Sangoot wondered aloud.

"Maybe Zamar can find out when she interrogates him. You were right by the way," the corners of Jaag's mouth lifted into a smile, "my wife is very late for work!"

Chapter Two

THE UNVEILING

After a very long time had passed, the assembly was called. The Voice proclaimed, "I will create one to rule the Earth for Me." The thing cringed and felt its heart sink. Shock first, then sadness, and finally rage washed over it. It knew that soon it would have to make true its vow to destroy the new creation. The thing was not alone in its confusion and disappointment; the whole assembly was puzzled. They called out with barely veiled defiance: "will You create a thing that will make mischief and shed blood?" The heavens vibrated as the Voice bellowed its response, "I know what you know not."

September 17, 2010 Touba, Senegal Eighth Day of Shawwal, 1431 AH

Zamar had flown back to the terrace after the bounty hunters dragged Nemacus into the interior of the prison. Now alone, her mind's eye replayed scenes from a life lived centuries ago. At the same time, she was confronted with the very present reality of her husband, the powerful warden of a hidden prison. She had been waiting for this moment for a long time. Now that it was here she did not know what to do. How would she tell her husband the truth? She knew he would be angry, but she also knew that he would conceal his anger from her.

"Come down from there Zamar," called Jaag. "We have a new prisoner for you to interrogate. Perhaps you know him. He is called Nemacus."

Lightly, elegantly, she floated down to the surface. Her white cloak undulating over her shapely form as she descended, Jaag was struck—as always—by her remarkable beauty. Jinn could often take beautiful form before the eyes of humans, but Zamar was among the few whose natural form was very pleasing to the eyes of men and jinn alike. She was almost jet black in appearance, with the slightest hint of red leather, or copper undertones. Her face was perfectly proportioned except for the eyes—too large and feline ever to be put on a human face. The subtle reddish hues in her otherwise coal black face were accented by the bright shocks of shimmery metallic copper hair on her brows. The same shimmering fire flowed from the top of her head. Her beautiful mane was covered by the vaporous hood of her flowing white cloak.

"Yes, I know him," Zamar's clear soft voice cracked slightly. "He's from my clan. He was once a commander in my father's army."

"How long ago was this?" Jaag asked patiently.

"It must have been more than two hundred years ago."

"And that's when you last saw him?"

"Yes, why?"

"I am trying to make sense of something Ben Al-Hajji said." Jaag's large head tilted slightly as he looked over his bride, as if a change of viewpoint would make the situation clearer to him.

"What did he say?" Zamar asked.

"He said that you would be able to tell me why they brought Nemacus to me instead of selling him to the highest bidder. He said it was for loyalty, and that you would know what he meant by that."

"I see." Zamar said quietly. "I am not sure I can know the bounty hunter's meaning. Nemacus was a faithful general to my father, the Sultan. My father saw in Nemacus a successful and powerful husband for his daughter."

"You were married before?" Jaag asked.

Zamar paused, choosing her words carefully. "I never married Nemacus. Though, if my father had his way, I would have. By the grace of God, I left home before the ceremony." Already, Zamar had said more than she would have liked. She began again, this time with impatience straining her voice. "It seems to me that the world of two hundred years ago matters little at this moment. We have a dangerous prisoner in our custody. I trust you will want me to interrogate him?"

"Yes," sighed Jaag. "Zamar, when you have finished, you must tell me the truth about your past. I have granted you peace and privacy out of respect and out of love. Now, the past is living here among us. It is divulging secrets that I would rather hear from you. Do you agree?"

"Yes, my husband, I agree," Zamar said. She regretted keeping secrets from Jaag. He was a good husband who deserved to know the whole story. Still, she was afraid that a full recounting of her past could signal the end of her future. She would tell him more, make her past less of a mystery. It was best that he didn't know everything—not just yet. Now, as she descended into the shadows of the prison hall, she faced a bigger concern. Just before her was Nemacus' cell. She couldn't see or hear him but she could smell his stench. She had searched for the truth for so long; it never occurred to her that a part of her didn't want to truly know what happened to her first family. So much time had passed that Zamar began believing that it was God's plan to show her the truth in the afterlife. But if it was so then why did God allow his capture? Why did He cause their paths to cross again after hundreds of years? She wanted to back away from the cell and have Jaag assign a new guard. Then, he spoke. "Who goes there?" That voice. That lisp. Hearing it revived an ancient hatred in Zamar.

Zamar moved closer and pulled the clay handles on the outside of the iron door, swinging it open. She stayed behind the door and out of sight. She affected a gruff raspy tone and a bellowing echo in her voice as she began to speak: "We are here to interrogate you," she said. From inside her cloak she drew forth a gold-colored ledger and opened it.

"We will commence with a series of questions." Zamar began, still projecting intimidation in her voice. "You must know, from the pain you have already endured today, that we are quite serious. If you wish to live another day, you will answer each of them truthfully, understood?"

Nemacus was in far too much pain to feel defiant, and this, along with his immobilized state made it impossible for him to match his interrogator's voice effects with his own. All he could muster was the word "yes" in his natural lisping hiss.

"What is your name prisoner?"

"I am called Nemacus."

"When and where were you born?"

"I was born among the jinn of the West, in the land the humans call Futa Toro. It was 476 years ago, in the three hundredth year of the rule of Sultan Nazreel."

"And, Nemacus is your name?" Zamar persisted, "your real name?"

"No," said the prisoner, forcing the words out from between hardened lips." My real name is Kasakasa. Nemacus was the name they gave me when I became a general."

"So, Kasakasa, do you have a spouse?" Zamar's voice broke ever so slightly over the word 'spouse' as the bellowing echo revealed the smooth crystal hum of her natural voice.

The prisoner remained silent. Zamar repeated the question, this time being certain to concentrate on projecting the rough and deep tone consistently.

"No," responded the prisoner, "I cannot say that I am married."

"Do you have any children?" Zamar asked.

"Yes. Many."

"How many?"

Nemacus paused to make his count before answering. "More than four thousand, but not one hundred more."

Zamar was stunned, but her voice held, and she continued: "More than four thousand? Are these your jinn children alone?"

"No. My jinn children are almost half that number. I cannot say for certain how many. I know that they must be outnumbered by the hybrids, but not by much."

"Why do you call the others hybrids?"

Nemacus chuckled stiffly in his hardened shell of a body. "Do not be naïve. They are the offspring of the two different breeds—human and jinn."

"Prisoner," shouted Zamar, "you know our meaning! Why call them hybrids here and not the name you call them in the market when you sell them? What do you call these?"

"They are called Elementals," replied Nemacus.

"Now we are getting somewhere! How many of these Elementals have you fathered?"

"Among the Elementals," lisped Nemacus, "one counts at least two thousand three hundred of my seed."

☪

Zamar had begun the interrogation with a dormant anger buried centuries deep inside her. Now it was vibrating, amplifying itself into a torrid rage as she listened to the monster speak. Images of her first family kept flashing across her mind.

Zamar was so angry that she feared that she would lose control. It would be so easy to veer off course and indulge her own passion and rage. But this would certainly cost her the chance of him disclosing everything. Zamar steadied herself once more and continued, "Do you know why you've been imprisoned?"

"I suppose my hybrid...sorry, my Elemental children have something to do with it, but honestly, I do not know."

"Do not waste our time!" Zamar was getting annoyed. "You know that you are wanted on three continents, don't proclaim ignorance now!"

"Perhaps you, unseen interrogator, should tell me why I am here," Nemacus hissed.

"Fine." Zamar bellowed in the echoing voice. "You are charged with malicious possession of fleshlings, manslaughter, murder, fornication, rape, sodomy, miscegenation, and *conspiracy*," Zamar answered coldly, lingering on the final charge. "It will be better for you if you confess your crimes."

Nemacus groaned deeply. "And, if I do, will you put me in a regular cell? The pain here is unspeakable."

"Be glad that you can speak, some are not so lucky." Zamar's heart flickered, remembering a time when a weaker prisoner, who was barely able to answer questions at all, suddenly expired in the middle of the interrogation. "We will consider a transfer only if you confess everything."

The prisoner, the most wanted jinn in the world, paused before asking wryly: "How will you know if I've confessed everything?"

"I will know." The words were gone and echoing in the air before Zamar realized that she had broken protocol. The impersonal "we" of the interrogator had given way, and she had answered the prisoner personally. She was still projecting that voice which seemed to come from everywhere and nowhere at once, but now Nemacus knew that his examiner was alone. He also knew that whoever was asking the questions had more than a passing interest in his case.

Nemacus scanned the doorway, his eyes tracking from left to right and said, "Come closer. I want to see you."

"No," bellowed Zamar.

"One cannot trust what one cannot see," argued Nemacus.

"Only those without faith reason thus," replied Zamar. "Besides, you have no choice. You must comply. I could shatter you to bits right now with that iron axe suspended above your head."

Nemacus tried to look up from inside his immobilized head. Though he could not see the axe, he was quite sure it was there. "I suppose you are right," he sighed, calculating. What would the truth cost him, after all? He could not be any *more* wanted. He was already the most hunted being on earth. Anyway, if there was even a slight chance that he would be moved from this iron cell, he was sure that he would be able to escape. He continued his response, slowly. "Well, let me start by saying I am innocent of the most recent charges against me. I did not kill that human."

"What then, are you confessing?" Zamar was growing increasingly impatient.

"When your bounty hunters found me," Nemacus paused before delivering the next words, "I was...*praying*. I was committing no crime."

Zamar scoffed. "And prior to those few moments of dubious spiritual reflection, what crimes did you commit?"

For what he said next, Nemacus summoned as much force as he could and spoke loud and clear, even managing to project a faint echo through the doorway and into the hall: "I will tell you what you wish to know, but only if we end this ridiculous charade. You will hear the truth from me, but only face to face, Zamar."

"When did you know?" asked Zamar, as she did what few jinn ever could and flew unperturbed into an iron cage.

"That's some trick," chuckled Nemacus, both stunned and strangely delighted at seeing a thing he thought impossible. "You always were full of surprises. This interrogation, however, was not one of them. I knew it was you all along."

"Even bound in iron and on the verge of death, you are still a liar, Nemacus." Zamar settled her feet on the iron floor and strode directly at her statue of a prisoner.

"And you are still beautiful and carry the scent of the sweetest frankincense. Tell me again why you did not marry me, Zamar?"

The coal-black jinniya leaned her face forward until her eyes were no more than a human finger width from his and stared at him with contempt. "No more games!" Gone was the false bass voice. Her echo was now stronger and it reverberated off the walls of the iron dome, humming like a crystal bell, "By God, you will speak truth or I will extinguish your flame here and now!"

☪

"I am a wearer of men." Nemacus began. "Few are better at it than I am. The last one I wore was a brute, already adept at deceiving the human women long before I flew into it."

"And what became of him?" Zamar asked.

"A woman took her vengeance on it. The woman came upon the man as it slept and pulled out its insides out with a sharp knife." Nemacus' mouth lifted ever so slightly at the corners into a hideously strained smile. "There was blood everywhere."

Zamar was disgusted, but she swept her finger across the pages of her golden ledger recording every detail. "Did you experience the life leaving his body?" she continued.

"That would be both dangerous and perverse now wouldn't it?" snarled Nemacus.

"It is still more twisted to fly into dead humans and animate them, yet I have seen you do this with my own eyes," Zamar snapped.

"No."

"No what?"

"No is the answer to your question. I left the lump of flesh before death came to take it."

Zamar was growing impatient with his insolence. But she expected nothing else from Nemacus, so she was annoyed but unmoved by his words. He could seek to prevail in debate if he wished, but she was the one gliding freely through his cell, battering him with questions. She gave silent thanks to God, for not making her wait until the Day of Reckoning to finally get answers from him.

She thought of the ledger in her hands, what it must record, and for whom. She slowed her pace and asked a question: "Tell me, Nemacus, how do you go about wearing a human?"

"You know this."

"It is a mere formality, for your trial, and for the record," she said raising the ledger before his eyes.

"Trial?" he scoffed. "When is this trial to be held?"

"That is not my affair, nor is it yours right now, you will answer the question or I will have you slowly broken into a thousand pieces."

"When I wear a man, or more rarely a woman, I put it on like a coat. I do not wear them nearly as much as I did before. It is exhausting and there is little sport in it anymore. They are all so very much the same. I fly into the nostrils and sit between the eyes. I must contract myself at first and stay lodged there. I begin to whisper deep in their ears. I am careful not to whisper too deeply or loudly at first."

"Why not?" she asked, waving her hands rapidly, though smoothly over the open pages of the ledger.

"They tend to go mad," he replied, grinning with his eyes. "I wasted countless of them when I was young and fiery. The weak would break. The strong ones would fight. They would seek protection and find means of driving me out. As the centuries passed I learned that it was much more effective to find that dark, soft place inside them and sit quietly for a while. They will show you the way. You will feel them vibrate with the thrill of sin. It does not to take long to learn their weaknesses. They are all the same anyway: lust, gluttony, pride…they are all being commanded to evil all the time anyway by something with their own selves."

Zamar interrupted, "You speak of the *nafs*."

"I have heard it called that," he continued. "Its name is not important. You speak with its voice at first; most cannot sense the difference. From then on you can command them without them even knowing it. They do not know to rebel. You only tell them that the evil they themselves desire is really good. Some of the fools even think that it is God talking to them! Almost all of them worship themselves like gods, so it matters little whether they take your voice for their own or for His!"

"Blasphemer!" shouted Zamar.

"Do you want to hear your answer or not?" hissed Nemacus. "Once your voice has taken over from theirs, you only need to feed the desires of their *nafs*, as you like to call it, to command them. You can have them do whatever you like with a mere word. You do not have to fight for control anymore, and you do not need to hide behind the eyes. They give you the whole body, limb by limb."

"Is this what happened to the brute you last wore?"

"Yes. He loved flesh and fornication, so I told him that he was right to love it. I told him that it was beautiful, and that the more of it he indulged the greater he would be. He did not even ask why."

"Did you drive him mad?"

"No. His mind was not broken when his wife killed him. It takes them years to go mad if you are patient this way, commanding the body without effort, instead of fighting them endlessly from a cramped space behind the eyes. And once you are in control you can make them go mad on purpose. All you need to do is command them to do a thing that cannot be undone. Make them the author of an act that their minds cannot accept and most of them break completely."

"How many of their minds have you broken? Two hundred? Three hundred?"

Nemacus scoffed and practically yelled, "oh, no!"

"Too many?" Zamar asked.

"Far too few! More than seven and a half hundred, but not eight."

"I see." Zamar was beginning to understand that hearing the truth from this monster was perhaps a thing best left for the Day of Reckoning after all. But she continued: "And what of breeding jinn with humans? You never fully answered my questions."

"I have mated with my share of human females before. Those days are behind me, now. I stay clear of humans and they of me."

"You have not answered the question, Nemacus," Zamar said, beginning to place the ledger inside her cloak and reaching towards the lever for the axe. "I asked you have you ever bred jinn with humans. Or, better yet, have you ever collected a group of jinn for the sole purpose of breeding them with creatures of flesh?"

"I do not wish to answer the question," he replied.

"Why? Because you have?"

"I do not wish to answer the question, because I fear that you will trigger that axe if you hear the truth."

"You devil! I will trigger this axe if you do not!"

"You know better than most, Zamar," Nemacus grinned knowingly, "that I am not the only jinn to have procreated with humans."

"Stop stalling Nemacus!" shouted Zamar, as she reached out and snapped off his left ear.

Nemacus screamed loudly, "You whore!"

Zamar went for his other ear.

"Wait, wait," he called out, whimpering. "This has always been a war, Zamar! I was a general, I only did what my sultan, what *your father* demanded."

Chapter Three

TAMKHARIT

The time had come. The Angels gathered as He blew life into the ornate figure that had so long been still just beyond the gate. Nothing like this had ever happened before. Every other thing He had made with a word, saying unto it "Be," and all at once there it was. This creature He had fashioned with His own hands, and here He was breathing into it His own spirit! The Spirit fought as it was forced into the clay form. The Voice said, "As you struggle to go in so shall you struggle to come out."

The Spirit journeyed on its reluctant course, and as it did, every dark and lifeless crevice within the figure came alive. Its eyes opened, its tongue moistened, it drew its first breath. Before the Spirit had even reached its waist, the man tried in vain to lift himself up. The Voice seemed to laugh as it proclaimed, "Truly man is made of haste!"

July, 1, 1764, Southlands of the Kingdom of Futa Toro, Senegal River Valley
First day of Muharram, 1178 AH

Alpha Ba lived in a world where entire villages vanished overnight. Today the dwellings of men had full granaries, glowing hearths, and laughing children. Tomorrow lame men and old women doused the huts and buried the dead. One settlement after the next was stripped of its people and consumed by fire. As long as people had a price, someone, somewhere, would succumb to greed and come to make slaves. Alpha sometimes lay awake at night, sure his village was next. Everyone had heard the stories of the coming of the *Cheddo*. They were always the same.

Sometimes they came slowly, sowing fear. The junior wives and the maidservants would be late coming back from the river or the well. When the young men made their way back from the fields as the sun stood at the top of the sky, they found the cooking pots were still cold. Frantic, the village would search for the missing. Most often they found nothing, and could only guess that their mothers and sisters, daughters and friends had been stolen and sold.

Sometimes a child, or a shepherd, or a wanderer would say that he had seen unknown men, Cheddo, in the tall grass on the way to the well. This was a sad mercy, for at least the village knew not to keep alive hope for their return.

All too often this was the shower that announced a coming storm. A day or two later the Cheddo would return in numbers and lay in wait. In the town's clearing, beneath its largest tree, the village would mourn its loss. Even as the married men and women of the village gathered in the light of the fire, a terrible assembly was gathering just beyond the ring of their huts. Once the tears dried and all the rumors had been heard, the villagers would deliberate their response.

"We should go to the sea and bargain with the whites for their return," someone would say.

"And who will protect you from the Cheddo on the road to the sea?" another would respond. "What will stop the white men from putting you in their boats?"

The debate would continue into the night—but whatever its resolutions, the men lurking in the tall grass would wait for the villagers to extinguish their hearths and go to sleep. Once the villagers' fires had cooled, the Cheddo lit their own.

The people awoke coughing. Smoke filling their lungs, they would rise to see their huts ablaze. Some roasted in their beds. Most leapt into action and tried to find a path away from the flames. Peering through the smoke in the flickering half-light, they would search desperately for their wives, for their children, for their machetes. Turning towards the woods at the edge of the village, they found that the flames had made a wall. A ring of fire and smoke, gunpowder and shot, closed in on them pushing them toward the main clearing of the settlement.

Under the tree where the village had shared the lambs of its feasts, where it had prayed together to break its fasts, where it had married its lovers, and named its children, they found a dreadful gathering. Here the town was assembled again for the last time.

Sometimes a Moorish mercenary presided over its end in Arabic, commanding his men, in the Holy language of the Qur'an: "Split the heads of the nursing children against the trees. They will not survive the ride. Put the larger ones in bags so they will not know their way home, and tie them tight to the horses."

Sometimes a white slaver directed the scene, straining his eyes in the inferno's false dawn to discern the young men from the aged. "Don't kill any more of the men!" he would shout in French or English. "Tie them up! And for God's sake don't waste any more shot on the old ones. Use your clubs, or just leave them to die."

But most of the time, the words the people heard at end of the world were in the tongue they had spoken all their lives, the one they learned—in the expression of the land—as they suckled. More often than not, it was a Cheddo chief who separated the men from the women, the young from the old, and those who would live from those who would die. He ordered the ends of lives and the beginnings of new ones in the common tongue of the land, for he too was its native son.

☪

Everyone had heard the stories. Alpha had watched this scene play out in his mind's eye many times. His uncle Wali was a powerful leader in a neighboring village and had sworn him protection. Alpha trusted his uncle, but he put his faith in God. He prayed that God would protect those who lived under his care. Alpha was sure the dream that kept coming to him at night after these prayers was a message from God. In fact, it seemed to him that this was more than a message. He was being given specific instructions, and a direct command.

In the dream, Alpha set out to leave on the first day of the month of Muharram, the first day of the New Year, and headed north to the Great River, passing through the Sogobe Forest on his way. Upon reaching the banks of the river, he followed its waters upstream toward the rising sun, and stopped at the first clearing. He saw a small girl sitting on a large rock seeming to wait for someone. As he grew closer, he could hear her sobbing. When asked why she sobbed, she responded, "Please make it go away. Only you can do it. Rid us of the river spirit. When it is gone this will be a place of peace." In the dream he saw a shape rising out of the water. He turned to look back at the girl, but she was gone. He raised the heavy stone on which she had sat and cast it at the being that was rising from the river. The rock fell atop the creature and splashed into the water. In the ripples after the splash, he could see "Peace Only" spelled out in Arabic letters, but with the language of Futa. *Jam Tan*. He then looked up, and on the opposite bank, he saw himself standing on the shore in front of a thriving village.

Alpha shared his dream with his wife and brother. They dismissed it immediately as a just a dream. But the dream would not leave him. It kept returning night by night.

Even though Alpha was still a young man, he was trusted with the business of the elders in his village because he knew the Qur'an by heart. He had studied some of the books of knowledge, and was wise beyond his years. Mostly, people listened to Alpha because he was a practical man, so part of him could not believe that he was readying himself to leave his wife and four children on this, the first day of the New Year to follow a dream.

He was practical, but he was also faithful. And in the end his faith won the day. For nearly a month, every time he opened his books of knowledge, they seemed to fall on the same words. "The Messenger of God—blessings and peace be upon him—said: 'a true dream is 1/27th of Prophethood." Alpha was being confronted by a true dream, offering him guidance from God, and a direct message from the Holy Prophet to follow it. He resolved that he would obey, over and against the protests of his family, and those of his own heart.

He promised his wife Sokhna, that he would return by *Tamkharit*, the tenth day of the year. The learned men and women of his land would fast this day and give charity to expiate their sins. This was a very weighty day, and it was best to be home when it came. In the books of knowledge it was written that this day, *'Ashura*, they called it, was a day of great tribulation for the people of God. It was the day that God forgave Adam and Eve for their sin, and it was also the day that he sent them down from the Garden to the Earth. It was the day that Noah's Arc finally came to rest upon dry land. God parted the Sea for Moses on this day and drowned the Pharaoh. It was the day that Jonas emerged from the belly of the fish, that Joseph escaped from the well, and that Abraham was saved from being burned alive by Nimrod. Some of the books said that this was the day that Enoch was raised to the heavens, and likewise Christ. This was the day of deliverance.

Nonetheless, the people celebrated this day of many trials. After sunset they visited one another and gave tidings of the New Year, sharing large bowls of meat and couscous made with the grain of the land.

For the children it was the best day of the year. As a boy, Alpha had enjoyed the disguises the children wore, as if to prevent the bad spirits from finding them. Like the other boys, he dressed in girls clothing, rimmed his eyes with kohl, and hung dangling rings from his ears. His brother Samba looked so ridiculous as a girl that he doubled over laughing every year as they got dressed.

The boys would then emerge into the courtyard and see that their aunts, nieces, and cousins had taken the soot from cooking pots and mixed it with water to paint their faces with false beards and moustaches. They would laugh at their pants, and belts, and turbans until tears rolled down their cheeks. Then, after sundown, they would all go door-to-door, singing songs, and begging for money, gifts, and especially sweets. The children would bring gifts of flour or sugar to their parents, but they kept all the sticky syrupy cakes, the fruit, the dates, the fried cakes dripping with honey, and gorged themselves into the night.

It was one of the very few pleasures he had as a child growing up in the age of the Cheddo. The Cheddo had stolen many children, but they had stolen childhood away from all. Gone were the days when parents let children run off and play alone, exploring the edges of their world. Everyone feared that they might be snatched up by Cheddo and sold to the whites. Sometimes when Alpha's mother returned late from the market, his wicked cousin Seydu would tell him that the white man got her. He was six years old before this stopped making him cry.

☪

So, on the first day of Muharram, as Alpha packed a small leather sack, his heart was filled with sadness that almost thirty years later, his chief concerns still involved the Cheddo. He was not small and helpless anymore. He was not the tallest man in his village, nor was he the strongest. But he was solidly built, quick-witted, and confident. As he had proven many times in wrestling matches, he had a way of handling himself. When he was young, before he went away to study the books of knowledge he was always the champion his village put forth in competitions with other towns. Before the combat, children would taunt him, comparing his firm yet ordinary frame with the tree-trunk legs and rippling muscles of their village heroes. But after those matches, the girls from those distant villages would make eyes at him, even though he was not the most handsome boy. His plain brown skin and ordinary features did not garner him that attention, it was his skill as a wrestler.

Sometimes the griots would make up spontaneous praise songs in his honor after a great victory against a gigantic opponent. They called him "Black David" and sang of his victory over Goliath, or they likened him to the "Desert Wind" wearing down the tallest towers. But Alpha's favorite was the song where he was re-named the "hand-axe." The chorus reminded the listeners that the most ordinary tool in the compound could fell the mightiest tree if used properly.

No, Alpha was not afraid. He knew how to handle a sword, ride a horse, and shoot a bow. He trusted in God and knew that he could handle himself. But now he had so much more to lose than before. Tonight *his* own children, Khadija, Momar, Khalifa, and Mariama, might cry themselves to sleep in fear that *he* might not return. He had just finished his morning prayer, but he found that he still had little peace about the decision. As he folded his prayer mat into his sack, and grappled with his own doubts about his plan, he heard his brother Samba call out in greeting.

"Salaam Maleekum elder brother!"

"Maleekum Salaam younger brother," replied Alpha, ushering Samba into the room. His brother was taller, sturdier, and darker-skinned. He looked much like Alpha, but with striking features that made him the more handsome of the two. This morning he carried with him a heavy trunk.

Samba placed the trunk down on the floor, before sitting down on the only piece of furniture in the room, Alpha's woven reed bed. Samba made all the necessary greetings and began the small talk. He was very good at small talk. Alpha was not. Alpha knew why he was there and was a little impatient. He knew that Sokhna had sent him one last time to try to talk him out of leaving. In spite of his frustration, he tried to speak well to his brother.

"Son of my beloved mother," he said, "I know why you are here. But my mind is made up. God has laid the path before me; I must walk it. I will return in ten days time at the most."

"Alpha, I have known you to take your time, but never to change your mind. Nonetheless, I hoped that this one time, you would reconsider. Futa is not safe these days, even for the people of knowledge."

"I know brother," he replied, "I will be careful. I assure you, this matter is decided, I have been given the gift of a vision, I must trust my Lord and follow it."

"I knew you would say that. That's why I brought this," said Samba tapping the trunk with his left foot. He unlatched it and reached inside, pulling out a large musket.

"My faith is my weapon," Alpha said thrusting the gun back toward his brother.

"Don't be a child Alpha! You're a fool if you don't take this gun!" Samba shoved it back.

"I'd be a fool to rely on anything but God."

"Would you be a fool with a bullet in your head? In your heart? Being dragged onto a slave ship is foolish. God wants us to protect ourselves. We should be armed at a all times."

"My armor is His word," Alpha said, tapping the Qur'anic talismans tied around his left shoulder.

Just then, Sokhna's voice called out in greeting. "Peace be upon you!" Alpha answered her and called her into the room.

"Peace Sokhna. Did you sleep well?" Alpha said politely.

"Yes. Praise God. And what are the brothers Ba up to this morning eh?" she said, smiling.

"I am sure you know what we are discussing," began Alpha, a little impatiently, "as it must have been you that sent Samba to me this morning. I never see him up and about at this hour!"

Samba slung the musket over his shoulder, and threw his free hand up. "I tried, Sokhna," he said. "Maybe you should tell him about your dream."

"No."

"Why not?" said Samba.

"It's been weeks since I had that dream. It didn't make sense then and it doesn't now."

"Tell me Sokhna, what was it?" Alpha asked.

"I don't give much credence to dreams. I can never tell if my dreams are from God or the Shaitan so I don't worry about them. But, I will tell you only in hopes that you can see what I could not. In the dream, you were squatting by a river to drink when a large lion attacked you."

Alpha and Samba waited for more. But Sokhna only looked at them.

"That's it?" Alpha asked.

"That's enough," Sokhna said.

"Well, that's not really everything," hurried Samba. "Tell him the rest. Tell him about the eyes."

Sokhna glared at Samba, for a moment, and then continued. "I yelled to you to get up from the river and that's when the lion noticed me. It rushed towards me. Even though it roared, I was fixated on its eyes. I could tell it knew something about me from its eyes. They were thinking eyes."

"I am not sure I understand, my dear."

"Oh Alpha, don't you see? This wasn't a normal lion. There was a thinking mind inside."

"Sokhna," began Alpha, "any animal that hunts, thinks. Besides, not all dreams are meant as a warning. In your heart you are afraid to let me go."

"Husband," she said sweetly and desperately, "come with me to see Ami. She can tell us what we need to know. She will know what to do."

"I already know what to do," Alpha insisted. "No magician can give me better guidance than I have already received from my Lord."

"Brother," interjected Samba, "it is not my place, forgive me, but how will it hurt to see what the woman has to say?"

"Yes…yes, there he's said it," stammered Sokhna, seeing an opening. "Besides, like your fathers, you have always been able to see hidden things. If Ami is false you'll be able to tell right off."

"You tempt me with pride," replied Alpha, gently yet firmly moving her aside to finish packing his bag. "And you, little brother," he said glaring at Samba, "after all we have seen you should know that God forbids magic."

Turning back to his wife, he paused for a moment, and then spoke. "You can't let your wants make you behave badly, Sokhna. God is watching. Always watching."

☪

Alpha loved Sokhna. The happiest day of his young life was the day he and his father went to ask for her hand. Sokhna's father, Njaga, had come to their village from Waalo, one of the neighboring lands of the Wolof people. He had come to study a book of law with Alpha's father, Amadu, bringing his young wife and small family in tow. He never left. He had come to like Futa very much, though he never learned to love the language of its people. Some of the small children would make fun of his heavy accent, but the adults respected him. He tilled his lands, studied his books, and took care of his family. Amadu liked him a great deal and would often receive visits from their family. Alpha seemed much older than Sokhna at that time. He was becoming a young man, wrestling, tending flocks, and learning books of knowledge. Njaga's little daughter played house in his courtyard and laughed louder than most. Alpha never had any reason to notice her, but she had every reason to look up to him. Soon he went far away to study.

While he was gone, Sokhna blossomed into a young woman. Before long, young men from all the neighboring villages began sniffing about her father's compound. They offered to run errands for him and brought him small gifts.

Sokhna liked the attention, and the new way the young men looked at her. Njaga did not. He also remembered that some were the same boys who had made fun of his hard tongue.

After a few years, Alpha returned. The day he came back, Njaga and his daughter were visiting. Alpha was carrying gifts for his mother and sisters from faraway lands, and precious books from faraway teachers for his father. He nearly flung them all over the courtyard when he saw Sokhna.

Having just climbed down from his mule, he unfastened the bundle and the wooden trunk that he had carried. He placed the chest on the ground and rushed to take the bundle in to his sister. There he saw her. His face went flush so quickly that he was sure she must have seen it. He did not know what to do so he turned to walk the other direction, tripping right over the trunk he had just placed on the ground.

Three weeks later, he came with his father to Njaga's door. He brought three bags of millet, a basket of cowries, a basket of kola nuts, a cow and three small rams. He wasn't wealthy, but he knew how to handle money and he knew that the woman was worth it. Sokhna refused to look at him. She only smiled shyly whenever he spoke. The wedding date was set for the first Friday of the dry season.

The night before the wedding was exhausting. He stayed up most of the night learning from his uncle in the ways of pleasing a woman. His brother Samba seemed to be curiously well-informed on the topic as well. It was too late to take a nap so his uncle broke a cola nut in half and gave them to Alpha to bite on. He put one in his mouth immediately. The bitter juice gave him a jolt. He rubbed the magenta underside of the unbitten half with his thumb, thinking of ways to open Sokhna like a flower.

☪

Sokhna had not fully realized how lonely she would be with Alpha gone. The first day came and went quickly, but the night dragged on for ages. Most husbands slept in their own rooms except when they wanted to make love to their wives. But the woven reed bed in Alpha's room was almost unused; he spent most nights with her, just to be close. Tonight, he was far away. She sighed and tossed in bed. Whenever tears welled in her eyes, she squeezed them away and bit down on her lower lip.

When sleep finally overcame her she dreamt again that a lion attacked Alpha as he squatted before a river to drink. She told her brother-in-law Samba the next day at lunch. "God willing, he will be fine," Samba assured her, "Alpha will return to you in peace and safety."

Sokhna wanted to believe him, but that night— Alpha's second night away— some traveling griots came to spend the night in the village. To payback the hospitality, they sat in the firelight and regaled the people with songs and stories. Some were old; some were new. One of the new stories sweeping through Futa was of a lioness that was killing people when they came to drink from the great river. Samba found his sister-in-laws eyes in the firelight. She was pulling away from the bonfire in tears. He prayed that God's will would not include his brother being eaten by a lion.

Chapter Four

FAMILY

When the Spirit reached the limits of the figure it doubled back, flying out the way It had come in, through the nose. The figure was now a living, breathing man struggling to stand for the first time.

The Thing emerged in the assembly just at this moment. It was furious. Perhaps it had not seen the kiss of life; perhaps it was this very kiss that had enraged it. Seeing the once hollow shell towering over the assembly was all too much. It remembered flying in an out of its dark insides for millennia. "That thing is empty," it growled to itself. "It will spend all of its life trying to fill that void inside it. That is how I will destroy it!"

April 18, 1742 Southlands of the Kingdom of Futa Toro, Senegal River Valley Twelfth day of Safar, 1155 AH

Zamar first met Alpha when he was only a little boy. The day that changed everything started like any other. For longer than she could remember the days seemed to be all the same for Zamar. She drudged through life as her father's scribe. She kept the ledgers for the great Sultan Nazreel. For half a millennium he had ruled over the jinn of the West. Her duties included chronicling the names of the humans her clan wore. According to her father, their ancestors had been wearing humans since the beginning of all things. After reading a few of the ledgers it seemed that her father spoke the truth.

In those books, she learned that her father's appetite for blood and misery was unmatched by most sultans of his kind. The humans they wore were vulnerable and almost always completely oblivious to that fact that they were being worn. All they knew was that they sometimes did not feel quite themselves. A few understood they were hearing voices, but did not know whose voices they heard. Some blacked out only to awaken covered in blood and forced to behold some awful thing their hands had done.

Zamar read too many stories about how The Wearers drank from pools of blood or dined in the waste of some poor human who died as a result of their possession. There were just so many volumes about the humans who lived and died in this land, some noteworthy, most not. All however, were recorded in the ledgers. Some were little more than names and timestamps, but especially when the entry was about a human who had been worn or influenced, the accounts contained a wealth of detail on the low, vile depths to which humans could sink.

Zamar never felt comfortable with her job, but for her it was better than the alternative—wearing humans. For as long as she could remember she found that whole business distasteful. This was unfortunate, since her father was the sultan of a tribe of jinn at the forefront of the war on humanity. Under different circumstances a softhearted creature like Zamar might have been cast out from her clan, or even killed. But she was the daughter of Sultan Nazreel and he gave her protection and a part to play in the family business.

She was bookish and had no taste for blood, so she kept the books. And on this soon to be extraordinary day, she was doing the most ordinary of things: recording the movements of her father's soldiers. Then something unusual happened: her father paid her a personal visit.

"How have you been, Zamar?" Sultan Nazreel's deep and smooth bass voice filled her small chamber before he even entered the room.

"Sultan?" replied Zamar, "is it really you?"

"Yes child, and please call me father," the Sultan bellowed, gliding across the threshold of Zamar's cave. "You are to wait outside," he said, addressing the dozen monstrously large jinn that served as his personal guard. As they retreated, he turned again to his daughter.

Zamar looked upon her father. He always frightened her a bit. He had not changed in any way that she could notice since she was born. He was a hulking jinn; angular and blockish as if he had been cut from a slab of rock. His pale grey color confirmed the impression. His head was nearly the size of his torso, and his elongated chin jutted forward. He had large curved teeth that kept his mouth from ever fully closing and made it appear at all times as if he was snarling at the world, which he usually was. He was so much different from her that as a child she sometimes wondered if they were really kin. But the metallic copper-colored eyes, eyebrows, and beard—which extended from Nazreel's chin nearly to the ground—made the family resemblance unmistakable.

"This is a surprise," Zamar said politely. "What brings you all the way down here? You've never been one for reading books."

"I have come on important business," he said lowering his pitch so that the sound would not reverberate off of the craggy walls of the cave. "You will not like it. However, in this situation I can turn only to you."

"What is this thing that I will not like?" Zamar was nervous; her father had long since stopped asking important things of her.

"You must go with Nemacus on an important mission," he said looking directly into her eyes to watch for her reaction.

"You cannot make me marry him. We went through this already, seven years ago. I spurned him, disobeyed you, and now none dare approach me for marriage. Is this not enough shame for the three of us already? Please do not send us down that road again."

"Silence child," Nazreel whispered, "this mission is not marriage. It is far more serious. And perhaps you will like the idea even less, but this time I cannot leave you a choice. I need you to comply."

"Please speak then sultan...father. Tell me what is this task that you have appointed for me?"

He glared at her with his hollow copper eyes before he began to speak. "Today the jinn have a chance to right an ancient wrong. Today we turn the war against the fleshlings once and for all." His voice had begun to grow, nearly filling the room again before he recalled that his speech was not to rally his minions for war, but to persuade his gentle daughter. He lowered his voice again and continued:

"For some time our seers have warned that one of Adam's seed was coming and that his arrival would have catastrophic consequences for our kind. The one of which they speak would live in their world, and would be able to see into ours. He will know our secrets and fight us with our weapons. They see disaster coming if he reaches the age of maturity. We came very close once to ensuring that he would never be born. Now we have a second chance."

"Father," began Zamar, "I do not understand. What does all of this have to do with me?"

"You, child, have been keeping the ledgers. Did you not wonder why we follow their births and deaths so closely? Some of them are more important than others. Some of them we need, because wearing them aids our cause. Others we leave alone or wear only for sport. And some of them…some fleshlings must be destroyed because they threaten our interests. We must watch them all closely, identify them, and count them. Knowing your enemy is critical in any war. You are intelligent, surely you have known this." He said raising one metallic copper eyebrow knowingly.

Zamar knew that her writing was never so harmless as she liked to believe, but to hear it like this jarred her. Nonetheless, she kept her flame from flickering in rage. "I understand. But this still does not explain why you need me now."

"I will get there in due time," said Nazreel impatiently. "There is much the seers do not see. There is much they cannot tell us. They did not know when or where this seed of Adam would be born. He may already walk among us. He may be born tomorrow, or in thirty-three years; or in three hundred thirty-three years. But they have pulled threads from the fabric of his time and they all seem to wind back to this one place. It is why we have been watching it so closely."

Zamar's insides were a whirlwhind. Her father's words were frightening her. She also felt a sudden thrill of discovery pass through her. It was all beginning to make sense. She steadied her flame and asked a question she was sure she already knew the answer to: "Is it the little village at the southern edge of Futa? The place of the teachers?"

"Yes!" Boomed Nazreel. "You are finally beginning to understand the ways of war! Know your enemy!" He laughed excitedly. "The seers are certain that the blood of our foretold enemy now flows through the veins of two boys in that village! They are the sons of one of its teachers. We have an opportunity…a duty to end that bloodline tonight."

Sultan Nazreel smiled. This was a thing that Zamar had not seen in some time. Then he began to speak again. "Zamar, I knew I was wise coming here. I knew that you only needed time, that you would change, that you would become one of us. You have always been special. Yes, very special indeed, and I need your special talent for this task."

Zamar cringed. She had stopped listening at the words "special talent." They hung there in her mind and pulled her back down a dark path to her childhood. Her ability to pass through iron, her imperviousness to salt, had been kept secret for as long as she could remember. Her father never let her show her gifts. He never let her speak of her special talent. It shocked her that he would speak of it now, even discreetly, especially with the guards only on the other side of the door and might still overhear.

Her father was still talking about how pleased he was, but Zamar only snapped back to reality when she heard him mutter derisively, "that fleshling village with their haughty 'teachers'. They have protections! Ha! My daughter has the gift, she will win us this war!" She interrupted him for the first time in her life.

"My sultan," she said, "you do not understand. I do know the village. Yet I still know nothing of the strategies of war. Like the little jinniya you knew, I still like books, and puzzles, and solving riddles. I saw a puzzle hidden in the coding of the ledgers, a riddle in the patterns of the entries. They all kept pointing to that place. I realized that the little village of teachers must be important. I have been watching it on my own for years now. I listened to the lessons. I heard them reading the Book."

Zamar paused, not sure her will burned bright enough to say the words: "Father, I have submitted myself to God. The old teacher from the village put me on the Straight Path two moons ago. I am a Muslima."

Nazreel's huge right hand sped toward Zamar's face so fast she had not even cringed when the blow found its mark. His fist cracked the cave wall just behind her left shoulder. "Curse you! You insolent little fool!" shouted the sultan. "Will you ever stop disappointing me?"

The sound of the blow brought two of the guards to the doorway where they peered in. A glare from Nazreel sent them back outside. He lowered his flame before turning back toward Zamar and speaking now in a cold, measured voice.

"I protected you from birth, when the jinn of all the continents sent their bounty hunters. Their seers must have seen that one with the gift had been born in our lands. They came to kidnap or kill you. I saved you. I killed the first ones to come with my own hands. I hid you and your gift away until they stopped looking for you. I made sure that no one would come and take your fire."

Zamar began to speak, but Nazreel closed his eyes and clenched his fists, and she knew to be silent.

"What you have said is treason. Treason is punishable by death. Fortunately for us both, no one else heard you. I am going to pretend that you never said it," Nazreel continued, "on one condition: You will accomplish this mission. *The teacher's sons die tonight or I take your fire myself.*"

☾

"No, I will not!" little Alpha screeched, trying desperately to wriggle out from under Samba's thick forearm. Samba was the younger of the two brothers by nearly two years, but he was bigger and stronger than Alpha.

"Come on," said Samba chuckling, "what, are you afraid of the dark?"

"Don't be stupid. Night has nothing to do with it. By God I wouldn't go there at high noon!"

"Please big brother. I need you to protect me," Samba said, using words he knew Alpha would respond to.

"You need *me?*" Alpha asked.

"Come on, of course I do. Besides, there is a calabash of jewels waiting for me, for us. It is more than one man can carry. I need your help. All we have to do is just go and get it." Samba said excitedly.

Alpha was unmoved: "Who's giving it to us?"

"You can't ask that. That's the only rule about it. We just have to go and get it." Samba said, releasing his hold on Alpha, but still blocking his escape.

"Samba," Alpha exhaled sharply as he said his brother's name, "there are people in the woods…there are things in the woods that might mean us harm. We could get snatched and never be seen again."

"Father has salt all around this village! There are verses of protection hidden in every house. You don't have anything to worry about."

"But Samba, we're not going to *be* in the village," Alpha protested. "You want us to go to the forbidden forest. Father says we are never even supposed to go near that forest and certainly not inside it."

"Father will be happy when he sees all the gold and jewels we've brought back. We will be princes of Futa, and he will be king!" Samba cried.

"If you think father will like the idea so much, why not go and tell him about it, hmm?"

"Don't be foolish. We can't tell anyone about it. It has to be secret."

"Who says so? And I thought you said there was only *one* rule. No asking questions, no one can know…who is making up all these rules anyway? Samba, who told you about this treasure?"

"I never saw him, but he knows lots of things about the village, about us…he knows what he's talking about. Look Alpha," Samba sighed, "I am going to get this treasure and you are coming with me, otherwise I will tell father that you were the one that was watching the goats when they ran off."

"You were watching the goats!" Alpha shouted.

"Father doesn't know that!" Samba teased.

Alpha was not bothered by Samba's silly threat, but he knew that there was no point trying to talk his brother out of a thing. It only made him want it more. If he didn't say yes, Samba would be talking a hole in the side of his head the whole night about that treasure. He measured the situation and resolved to follow his younger brother toward the woods and then, at his first chance, he would make a run for it back to the village. When Samba was out in the dark, near the forbidden woods, he would turn and run back to the village too. That would be the end of it.

"Fine. I'll go," Alpha said wrapping his prayer beads around his wrist. "But I won't go unprotected." He reached under his bed and grabbed the old rusty iron machete the boys used to cut down plants and skin cane rats.

"No weapons! He said no weapons," Samba protested.

"So now there are three rules? I'm not going out there without a machete," Alpha insisted.

"Fine, you take your protection, I'll take mine," said Samba, reaching under a stack of folded cloth to retrieve a black braided necklace with a small leather pouch sewn closed with gold thread. "Where did you get *that*?" Alpha asked. Samba slid the necklace over his head. The pouch rested in the middle of his chest.

"From no one you know," Samba replied.

"Can you trust the one who made it?

"More than I can trust you," Samba said laughing.

Alpha was not laughing. "That's not possible," he said, "I'm your brother."

☪

The settlements of men were made up of rings. Rings within rings. The boys were venturing outside of the circles their mothers and fathers had traced to keep good things in and bad things out. They quietly slipped out of their round hut. They stole away from their circular family compound. And as they exited the village, Alpha noticed that it too was ringed with a circle of ten massive baobab trees.

Samba led him further away from the village, from the safety of their father, and from the protective barriers surrounding his people. Alpha fingered his prayer beads nervously, *la ilaha illa Allah*, there is no god but God, he said repeatedly. It was almost the middle of the month and the moon was bright in the sky. On nights like these, the light-brown sands shimmered brightly in the moonlight, making the paths of men appear to glow. Though tonight just as the boys left the village, the moon had hidden behind gathering clouds. The world was dark, and in spite of whatever he may have said, Alpha was still a little bit scared of the dark. "Samba, how much farther is it?" Alpha asked.

"It can't be far now. We are almost there. Just a few more steps and we'll arrive. I'm sure of it," Samba replied. They were now no longer on the paths of men; they were making their way through a thick forest.

"You said that way back there," Alpha said before he stopped walking. "Samba, I think we should go back. How do you know it was not a slaver whispering lies to you in the woods? How do you know it was not a jinn? No one gives away treasure for nothing. Have you thought about what they may want in return?"

Samba abruptly turned around. "You have no nerve! How can father always choose you over me?"

"What are you talking about Samba?" Alpha said in a voice that was a whisper and a shout at the same time.

"Father has no favorites, only children. I am going back to tell him what you've done."

Alpha turned and started to make his way back to the path. The moon had come out again from behind the clouds and he could still see the way back to the clearing. Samba turned to chase his brother, "wait, Alpha, don't go. We're almost there. We'll have a treasure so great that no one can count it! We'll be rich!"

☪

At that very moment, a hissing voice called out faintly. "Saaaambaaa. Saaaambaaa." It seemed to come from everywhere and nowhere at once. "Is that you child?"

"Yes." Samba answered, turning his body this way and that to try to find the source of the sound. The braided necklace thumped against his chest each time he turned.

"Samba, don't answer! You can't see who you are talking to," Alpha whispered loudly.

"Shut up! I can't hear," Samba said. The voice now seemed to be coming from behind them, deeper in the woods and away from the road. Samba spun about and walked toward it. "Kasakasa, is that you?"

Nemacus, still veiled from human sight, floated down from the treetops and settled on a rock a few steps away from the boys.

Alpha felt a chill at the back of his neck and shuddered. He looked from side to side desperately straining to see the presence that he knew he felt. "Samba, this isn't right. This is all very bad. Don't go over there!"

Samba ignored him. "Kasakasa?" he asked as his eyes scanned the trees in the halflight. "I brought my brother to help me carry it," he said pointing to Alpha as he turned his head to see if anyone was there to see his gesture. "I did as you said. Where is the treasure?"

"It is just over here my child, come closer," Nemacus hissed, "you will have your reward for what you have done."

"I am ready," Samba gasped. He was out of breath from chasing his brother. His heart was pounding from the night's excitement. His chest heaved as he inhaled deeply to catch his breath. The charm around his neck swung back and forth across his chest like a pendulum, it's gold threads started to glow. The boy's mouth was agape. In flew Nemacus.

☪

Zamar watched the scene unfold, unsure of what to do. She saw Nemacus leap from his perch upon the rock, unfold into a spiral of vaporous mist, climb up the braided charm and enter into Samba's mouth. The boy's body jolted. His knees buckled and he began to stagger forward. He reached out and stopped his fall by bracing against the very rock that Nemacus had stood upon. He collapsed on it, seemingly unconscious.

Zamar was still cloaked from human sight, but just in case she had hidden herself behind a large termite mound a few steps away from Alpha. It was her turn.

She had gone her whole life without ever wearing a human and did not want to start now, but her father certainly would not hesitate to kill her if the mission failed. She remembered the old teacher said that possessing people was forbidden to believing jinn, and she had never wanted to try it anyway. Nevertheless, here she was in the forest as Nemacus put her father's plan for fratricide into motion. She felt that she had no choice. She leapt atop the mound and down at Alpha, her body whipping into a whirlwind as she approached his mouth. Just as she was about to enter him she felt a blinding pain pass through her and she felt her airy form being hurled to the ground.

She looked up at the boy, confused at her failure. The moon had just reappeared from behind the clouds. She could now clearly see that his vest was laden with talismans. His arms too. They were tied around the bottom of his shoulders. There was one around each ankle, and had she been able to see under his pants legs she would have seen another tied around his right thigh. They were of all sorts. Little pouches of leather, small brass cases, metallic bands with engraved words. The largest one was a silver diamond-shaped talisman that hung at the end of a chain around the boy's neck.

Now she understood. After years of watching the village she had seen the teachers make hundreds, even thousands, of these. Inside those pockets of metal and leather were small folded pieces of paper with hundreds of Arabic letters written on them—verses from the Qur'an, prayers of protection, calligraphic words with numerological secrets. Zamar had stared at the boy for several seconds before she realized that he was staring back!

She looked down at herself and realized that when she was repelled from entering him she had fallen to the ground in her natural form. The little boy was staring directly into the large cat-like eyes of a coal-black jinn with bright copper hair! Their eyes locked for only a moment, but it seemed like an eternity. Alpha shook his head rapidly to bring himself back. His stunned expression gave way to a fierce determination. He grabbed the iron machete from his hip, closed his eyes, and swung as hard as he could at the creature laying at his feet. She vanished.

Just then Samba's voice called out to him, very calmly, and with the slightest lisp. "Alpha, what was that? Are you alright?"

"There is no god but God!" Alpha exclaimed. "Little brother, I think I killed it. I mean…I think I saw it. I don't know. We have to get out of here."

"Calm down. You're seeing things. It's dark. Your mind is playing tricks on you," Samba began to walk toward Alpha with his left arm behind his back.

"Stop it. Shut up. This is madness. I am going home and you are coming with me," Alpha reached out and grabbed his brother's right arm.

☪

Zamar's flame flickered with fear and roared with excitement as she lay behind the termite mound. Alpha had not missed her. Caught in her natural form, she had been unable to dissolve herself as long as human eyes were upon her. Locked in place by his gaze, she had seen him raise the machete high and swing it down at her. The boy had closed his eyes just before the moment of impact, allowing her to disappear, but by then it was too late. Only her head and chest had become mist and begun to twirl away when the blow ripped right through her upper thighs. Any other jinn would have been cut in half. Except the blade passed right through her.

She looked herself over to be sure that she was still in one piece. Realizing that she was, she looked back at the boys. She saw Nemacus' eyes where Samba's should have been. She also saw that there was a plan in place in case she had lacked the nerve to possess the older boy and have them slaughter one another. Nemacus had used Samba's arm to grab a large jagged rock. She immediately knew what he was planning, because she had seen his favorite method recorded many times in the ledgers. He was going to kill Alpha anyway, gut him, and cover himself in the boy's entrails. He would then begin eating his flesh before awakening Samba to the taste of his brother's liver on his tongue. The boy would go mad on the spot.

☪

Alpha grabbed his brother's right arm. Nemacus raised Samba's left arm to strike. Zamar was not sure why she did what she did next. But she knew that this thing that was about to take place had to be stopped. She leapt into a mist again only this time twirling toward Samba. Zamar entered the body of a human for the first time.

Just as Nemacus brought the rock swinging down at the crown of Alpha's head, Samba's body jolted again as the jinniya entered him. She was too late. There was a loud crack as the stone hit Alpha's head and he fell to the ground with a bloody gash opening along his temple. The blow had not split Alpha's skull as Nemacus intended, still he lay on the ground unconscious.

Samba lapsed in and out of consciousness as two jinn struggled for control of his body. Zamar had always hated Nemacus. And Nemacus had always underestimated Zamar's strength of will. After only a few moments, Samba was doubled over vomiting out a grey vaporous mist that fell to the ground in front of him like a heavy fog. As it touched the ground it solidified into the form of Nemacus.

Zamar knew what to do. She extended Samba's arm and fumbled for the iron machete laying next to Alpha's unconscious body, all the while keeping her human eyes fixed on Nemacus so that he would not be able to vanish.

Not experienced in the wearing of humans, she struggled with the weight of the machete as she lifted it above her head. She swung the boy's arm clumsily at Nemacus' head but missed wildly. He howled nonetheless as the blade ripped through his right hand severing it just above the wrist.

She struggled to raise the blade again. She would be rid of Nemacus once and for all. As she lifted it above her head—more quickly and powerfully this time—the tip of the machete cut through the black braided strap that held the charm around Samba's neck in place. The spell began to break almost instantly. She began to feel Samba struggling to take his mind back. Without the polluted charm clinging to his body, all the talismans that Samba's father had tied to the boy were beginning to do their work, forcing her out of his body.

Instinctively, she flew out from him before he overpowered her. Whirling out of his right ear, she quickly took the form of a creature she had worn many times before. She beat her wings as rapidly as she could and did not look back. Samba rubbed his eyes and looked up just in time to see the silhouette of a large owl as it passed across the moon.

☪

Samba ran as fast he could back toward the village. His heart pounded in his chest. He had never seen so much blood. His mind raced. Alpha is dead! Isn't he? He wouldn't wake up. My God! What have I done? When he arrived the moon was hidden behind the clouds and it was still hours before the first light would appear in the sky. The world was black and nothing was moving.

"Father!" he gasped, pounding at the wooden door to his father's earthen hut. A moment later Amadu emerged wiping sleep from his eyes. He assumed his son had been awakened by a bad dream, so in spite of the hour he made a comforting face and called his youngest son by his nickname.

"Soldier! Hey, what are you doing up son? Nightmare?" Amadu asked.

At this Samba began crying. "Nightmare? Father…nightmare…it's…no. I mean, yes. Only it's no dream. Daddy. Alpha!"

"Son," Amadu said, now wide awake and worried. He mumbled a prayer underneath his breath before continuing, "You are not making any sense. Don't rush your speech. Where is Alpha? Where is your brother?"

"It's all my fault. I made a terrible mistake," Samba shouted.

"What is all your fault son?" Amadu asked in measured breaths. He struggled to cap the fear and frustration welling up inside him.

"We went to the forest. I mean I went. I took him. I made him go. The man told me to bring him."

"Which forest? What man?" shouted Amadu, confused.

"The forbidden one. The man said come to the forbidden forest, and bring my brother to help me carry back the treasure."

"My God!" Amadu gasped, immediately thinking that a slaver had taken his son. "Samba where is Alpha!" he shouted.

"Father, Alpha is in the woods. I think the man hurt him. He won't wake up. I don't know what happened…there was blood."

Amadu pulled his knee length tunic over his head and pulled up his pants, tying the rope belt tight. "You better pray my eldest son is alive!" Amadu roared grabbing Samba's with his left hand, and pulling a large cutlass from behind a trunk with his right. "Take me to him! NOW!"

☪

Ayssatu, the boys' mother, slept lightly two doors away until she was awoken by the sound of her husband shouting and her son sobbing. She had actually been awakened an hour earlier by what she thought was a stomachache. She uncovered the earthen jar in the corner of her room and drew a cup of cool water to soothe it. Once awake, she realized that it was not her stomach, but her womb that ached. She opened the wooden shutters on her window and looked across the courtyard at the huts of her sons and daughters. Everything was silent, so she went back to bed.

Now her womb ached again at the sound of her son crying. *Which one was it?* She wondered. She had not heard either boy cry since they were very small. She covered herself with a large loose fitting bubu and opened the door to her hut to see the man and boy in fits at the door of his hut.

It was Samba. She should have known. Her voice was a whisper and a shout as she called out to them. "What's wrong?" She slipped her sandals onto her feet as she left the hut and began walking over to them. She knew it was something serious from the wild look in Amadu's eyes. She had begun to cry as he explained what happened.

Now she was pacing the courtyard, frantically thumbing her prayer beads, sure that she had already lost a son. She prayed that she would not lose the other, or even her husband.

☪

The first light was appearing in the sky and they still had not returned. Sounds were starting to come from the huts in the compound. At the center of the village, at the little earthen mosque the man was just beginning the call to prayer. "Allahu Akbar, Allaaaaaaaahu Akbar!" *God is still great even if He has taken my son*, Ayssatu sobbed to herself. "Ashahadu al la ilaha illa Allah!" the muezzin called out. *And I must still bear witness that there is no god but Him, even without a husband.* Ayssatu fell to the ground and covered herself in tears; her sobs drowned out the rest of the call to prayer.

But just as the muezzin began the final *la ilaha illallah* she felt a hand upon her shoulder. She looked up and saw Samba. Standing behind him, she saw her husband covered in sweat, carrying Alpha in his arms. The boy's chest heaved ever so slightly up and down. Ayssatu thought she was dreaming. Samba helped her to her feet. She kissed him, and then smacked his face as hard as she could.

"Mama I'm sorry," Samba cried, "please forgive me. I'm so sorry." Samba was crying and caressing his brother's head.

"Father, will he be alright? I'm so sorry. Please forgive me, I don't know what happened." Just then, Alpha opened his eyes. At this even Amadu could not stop a tear from rolling down his cheek.

"God willing," Amadu said breathlessly, "he will be fine. Now go make a full ablution before the prayer."

"And when you are finished praying," Ayssatu added, "go to the tree in the middle of the compound and get me a heavy switch."

☪

Across the savannah and through the forest, Zamar flew. She rested on a tree branch that hung over the Senegal River and sat there to watch the sun rise and set again. On the morning after watching the seventh sunrise, a group of women with their children approached the river. It was clear from what they carried they intended to bathe in the river. Zamar did not want to be bothered with any more people. She only wanted to scare them away but ended up starting a legend when she grabbed the ankles of two of the women while they waded in the water. They thought she intended to drown them. They told everyone back at their village and for a while Zamar had peace. A rumor spread that a dozen girls had drowned at that spot in the river. Over the next twenty years, Zamar's stretch of the river gained the reputation of being haunted.

Chapter Five

ALPHA & THE LION

How could he bow? It was impossible. The thing had only ever bowed its head to God. Now He was being commanded to bow down before this wretched mound of dirt! Why? How could He ask this? There was not a spot on the earth where the thing had not touched its head in prayer. It had glorified God on every mountain and in every valley. It had hovered over the depths of the seas and pondered the magnificence of Him and His creation. It could not bring itself to bow to any other.

It felt humiliated. And now the Voice proclaimed that this man…was to rule the earth. "No! The earth belongs to me! I should rule it," he thought.

They were told to call him Adam. Like the thing and its kind, it had been given the gift of choice. It could obey or disobey. At this moment the thing made of smokeless fire made a choice that could never be undone.

Alone in a sea of the prostrated forms of angels stood this jinn—a thing made of smokeless fire—proud and defiant. He pronounced what he had known in his heart for some time— that he would never bow to Adam and that he could only be his enemy. He promised that he would lead him and his descendants on the path of destruction. He swore to lay in wait for them and to attack them from the front and from behind, and to prove that man was a useless and ungrateful servant, certainly unworthy of dominion over the earth.

God, who is never surprised, gave him respite to do just that before He cast him out.

July 6, 1764
The Senegal River Valley
Sixth day of Muharram 1178 AH

Zamar had passed years praying, eating, and sleeping alone in the woods along the banks of the Senegal River. Most days, she took no form at all that people could see. One day during the dry season a lioness and her cub walked down near the riverbank to drink. She had never worn a lion before and was curious. The old teacher said that she was forbidden to wear humans—no one said anything about animals. She entered the lioness' body, arched her powerful back, and sharpened her claws on a stone near the riverbank. The cubs cowered away from her and growled, so she left the body of the lioness alone and flew into a tree to watch them play.

Eventually more people came. More people always come. They tried to settle along her bend of the river. Zamar was finished with people; she was finished with other jinn; she just wanted to be left alone. But the children of Adam saw sparkling water and lush ground, and the rumors of a haunted river were not enough to keep them away. They wanted this place for themselves. Zamar did not want them there, and she did not want to leave. After what she had done she could never go back to her kin. She had no place else to go. This bend in the river was a place of peace and a place of solace. It was her place.

Zamar remembered what being a lion felt like. When the people came to drive her out she took the form of a lioness, only larger. Just seeing her prowling the banks was usually enough to get them to go away. And sometimes they persisted, especially the young men who thought they could have songs sung in their honor if they killed her. They attacked her with spears, and swords, and bows, and guns. They set traps for her. Sometimes they came at her in number. She was forbidden to kill humans without reason; she knew that. But no one is forbidden from killing in self-defense. Once, she killed a man. She did not eat him, she only left him to rot in the hot sun. Eleven moons later, the sun was setting and she could smell another human approaching.

Will they ever learn? Instinctively, she became a lioness. A tall, solidly built man headed for the river. He looked familiar to her somehow, so she watched him first. He dropped his bag and spear beside him and crouched before the river. Cupping his hands he gulped down several handfuls of cool water. Never once did he seem afraid. She was confused. *He must have heard the stories about the lion that haunted the river. Why was he here?*

He sat as if he did not care about rumors or legends. Zamar crept closer. He drank so much of her water that it poured down his face. She was too quiet for him to hear but feel her he might. She suppressed the strength of her breath. And it must have been that unnatural action that caught the man's attention. His spine straightened, forming a rigid column. His right hand, dripping with water, slowly reached for his spear beside him. He rose and pivoted, pointing the tip of the spear inches from her face.

"It's true," he gasped. "I can't believe it's true." He panted and struggled to regulate his breath. His eyes were wild and intense. "I am not afraid, God. Please protect me."

Zamar could not help but notice the long scar running along his right temple. He widened his stance by shifting his weight to his back leg. He said a prayer and spat upon the ground. He did that three more times and never in the same place. He charged at her like a hunter. He jutted his spear at her until the tip of the spear grazed her forehead. Zamar roared a warning, but still he approached jutting the spear. She jumped to the side of him, took the handle of the spear in her mouth, yanked it from him, and snapped it in two. Horrified, the man stepped back and balled up his fist when most men would run.

"I've heard about you," he said. "I am not afraid. I am Alpha. By God, I will defeat you."

She lurched at him, gnashing her teeth. He struggled to stand when Zamar pounced on him with all of the strength and agility of a lion. Alpha crumpled under her. His forearm and elbow lodged in her neck. "I am Alpha. If it please God, you will succumb," he said. Zamar inhaled sharply about to roar, in that briefest of moments, Alpha said his most powerful prayer and spat in the lion's mouth. The lion froze. Her two hind legs extended out behind her. Alpha continued to pray as he climbed out from under her. Alpha continued to pray before spitting on her and everywhere he spat, Zamar's guise dissipated. Then he began to recite from the Qur'an rapidly. The Sura of the Jinn, the Fatiha, the Throne Verse, and other special passages he had learned from the books of hidden knowledge.

Zamar felt her arms and legs lose strength. The more he prayed over her, the weaker her arms and legs felt. He overcame her and tossed her over onto her back. Her mane began to shrink and so did her head. She looked at her paws and saw that they weren't paws anymore. They were now slender jet-black hands. She fought harder to resist the shift. Her mane came back and so did some of the power in her legs. Then Alpha began saying words she had never heard before. She instantly lost all lion form and was now her natural self, a four-foot tall coal-black jinniya laying in the arms of a six-foot two inch brown-skinned man. For the second time in twenty years, their eyes locked.

"It cannot be!" Alpha exclaimed. "I have seen you in a dream! A very long time ago, when I was a child."

He closed his eyes and rubbed them with the backs of his hands to make sure he was indeed seeing what he thought he saw. As soon as he broke the gaze, Zamar vanished into the night.

"No! Wait!" Alpha cried out. "Do not go! I will not harm you! Come back, I beg you!"

Zamar was stunned. She looked at the scar on his face. *Was this really the little boy she had saved on the night that everything changed? What was the meaning of this? How could he have returned? Why was God bringing their paths together once again?* In that moment she made a decision that would change both of their lives, forever.

She remembered the feeling of wearing a human, the feel of the human body, and the weight of it. She had also watched them closely for a long time. She knew their forms well. The teacher had forbidden her from wearing humans. All of these years, she had been trying to do what she was taught. She knew God was watching. She knew that before she had come to Islam even her bookish life of recording the wearing and killing of humans had earned His displeasure. She did not want to further displease Him now; for twenty years nearly her only sin had been occasionally striking fear into His servants so that they would leave her alone. Zamar had sworn to abandon all that was forbidden to her; but the teacher had not forbidden her to take the shape of humans.

☪

Alpha cupped his hands on the sides of his mouth and called out as loudly as he could. "Please! Come back! Who are you!" he cried.

"Peace be upon you son of Adam. I am called Zamar," a clear crystalline voice answered from directly behind him. Alpha turned about and saw a tall, slender dark-skinned woman standing in front of him. She stared at him from behind beaming bright copper colored eyes. He could only stare back into those eyes, knowing that he had looked upon them before.

He untied himself from her eyes and took in her whole face. He was looking at a woman with high cheekbones, slightly feline eyes, and slim dark eyebrows. Her nose was thin along its ridge before flaring lightly at delicately curved nostrils. The corners of her perfect mouth drew her full lips into a faint smile. Her face was exquisite—delicate, strong, and above all stunningly beautiful. Wild thick waves of reddish-copper hair tinged with flecks of golden-brown fell in curls over her shoulders. His eyes followed her hair down to her shoulders, and over the rest of her undulating, graceful, enticing form. He had looked over every inch of her down to her knees in a brief yet never-ending moment before he realized what he was seeing.

Then he stopped. He felt the blood rush to his face and was overcome with shame when he realized with his conscious mind that the woman was completely uncovered! He cast his eyes at the ground and tried to speak.

At first his throat made no sound at all, then he managed to choke and stammered his response to her. "And, peace be upon you Zamar. I am called Alpha," he said. "Do you not wish to cover yourself?"

Zamar was confused and suddenly embarrassed. She covered her nakedness with her hands and arms, and she folded her knees together. "I have no garment," she said, exasperated.

Alpha fumbled around in his leather sack and pulled out a thin woven cotton tunic. "This is all I have, you may take it," he said, extending his arm with his head tucked against his shoulder to keep himself from seeing her naked form again.

"Thank you," she said, "it is a…good…garment." Zamar struggled to put together the words of Alpha's language. She had lived around and among his people for more than a century; she understood their words well and read their way of writing even better. But she had not spoken to anyone, human or jinn in twenty years. She felt awkward. She pulled the tunic over her head. It came down to just below her knees.

"You have eyes and hair the color of fire," Alpha said, looking up slowly. "I've never seen a woman like you before."

Zamar lowered her eyes a bit as she started to speak. "I am not from this place. I am from the ocean…the city at the ocean, the city of the men with white skins. I was bathing here in the river. I saw you fight the lion."

"Is that so?" Alpha asked, smirking.

"Yes. Please forgive my…uncovering. You surprised me."

Alpha laughed so loud that his shoulders shook.

"You are not from the city of the whites!" he chuckled.

"I am," insisted Zamar, "How do you know? Have you ever been there? It is a strange place, different from Futa."

Alpha was amused, but he was finished playing along. "What you say is true; I have never been there. And it is also true that their ways are strange. However you are not a woman from the ocean or from the city of the whites, or from anywhere. You are not a woman at all."

"I don't understand," Zamar cooed.

"You are the lion. You are the little jinn in the cloak. I saw you just now and I saw you twenty years ago. By God, I had convinced myself it was a dream." Alpha lowered and shook his head as he spoke; he was talking more to himself than to the strange woman.

"A what? A jinn? Do not be crazy!" Zamar smiled.

"Zamar," Alpha sighed, raising his eyes to meet hers again, "enough games. I know you are not a woman. You are marvelous, almost perfect, but your feet are on backwards!"

☪

Zamar marveled greatly at Alpha. To her it seemed only yesterday that this boy stood his ground in the forest against the terrible Nemacus. Now he had come to her river and subdued her. *What was in this man that made him capable of all this?* She could not be taken with iron, salt, or fire. No man could match the strength of her lioness. No jinn she had ever seen could do the things she could do. And yet this child of Adam had taken her. He had defeated her with words, God's words. She could feel God watching. She knew He was bringing them together; she knew their destinies were woven together.

She stared at Alpha at length. He was a beautiful man. He did not overpower her with beauty at first; his features were not extraordinary. His nose was neither too broad, nor too slim. His eyes were neither large nor small. The longer she looked at him, the more she was drawn to him. He was tall and solidly built, but he was not an overly large man. His skin was the color of the earth of Futa, a plain brown at first glance, and as the halflight of the night shifted, she could see hidden in it tones of deep red clay, rich black soil, and light brown sands. The skin on his face was perfectly clear, except for the long scar along his right temple. His chest and shoulders looked not as though they had been chiseled from the hard stone cliffs at the bank of the river, but rather like they had been carefully carved from the softer limestone. His body was firm yet supple. This she knew from their wrestling match. Alpha's beauty did not overwhelm. After studying him she realized that the beauty in him was in perfect balance and proportion.

"I am sorry, Alpha," she said. "It was only play. I knew that I could not deceive you."

Alpha studied her face closely, the night winds of Futa blew cool across his body. It was only the beginning of the rainy season, and the heat had not yet come. At night one could still taste the chilly air of the Sahara desert blowing over the savanna and toward the river. "It is late, and it is getting cold. We must seek shelter for the night."

Zamar peered over the banks of the river to the north and saw at a distance what Alpha could not. "You are right child of Adam. The sand wind is blowing in the desert; soon it will blow here. It will bother your fleshy body. I can lead you to shelter, but you must come willingly. Do you wish to come with me?"

Alpha looked into her eyes and answered the only way he could: "Yes," he said, pulling the sack over his shoulder. "Which way to the path?" he asked.

Zamar laughed so wildly that Alpha could see the teeth at the back of her mouth. He would not have noticed at first, but they were just a little too pointy to have been human teeth. "There is no road to get to this place," she said as she began to slip out of the cotton tunic. "Hold this please," she said. He lowered his gaze and began to put the garment into his sack.

"Just pull your arms in tight to your body, take a deep breath, and try to stay calm." Zamar said.

Alpha did as he was told. The woman became like whirling grains of sand before his eyes, then she was something like a twirling spiral of smoke. The column of mist wrapped itself around him enveloping him completely and lifted him off the ground. Before he knew it she had whisked him out over the great river. Zamar followed its course upstream and around the bend before veering hard to the right. She flew up the mouth of a small tributary that flowed into the river, and after following its course a short way they came to a small waterfall in the little river. The water tumbled thirty feet over solid rock into a small pool before continuing on its way to join the Senegal. Alpha's heart began to beat rapidly as he saw that he was being carried directly into the waterfall's solid rock wall. Before he could say a word, the small tornado splashed through the wall of water and through the tiny mouth of a cave hidden by the cascading falls. The tornado began to whirl a bit more slowly around him now, about three feet off the floor of the cave. Suddenly the wall of wind retracted and dropped him on the stone ground of a very dark cave. He looked up and the beautiful, gracefully built woman was before him once again. He quickly reached into the sack for the tunic.

"I would have preferred a carpet ride," Alpha said laughing.

"I do not understand," said Zamar.

"It's just that…people say that…flying carpets," Alpha stammered, "It's not important. Listen, Zamar, there is so much that I want to ask you. It was you, wasn't it, that night in the forbidden woods? What happened to me that night? It wasn't you that attacked me was it? There was something else there. Why did you take the shape of a lion? How do you change shapes like that?"

"Alpha, I cannot answer all of these questions. I do not know the answers to some of them. To answer others might take a human lifetime. What I do know is that it is miraculous that we are talking together now. That we should meet again at all is a very mysterious thing."

"I am sorry, Zamar. I do not mean to trouble you suddenly with many questions. My people are curious. When there is a problem, we look at it from this side and that until we put it all together."

"Like a puzzle!" Zamar exclaimed with childlike joy.

"Yes!" Alpha smiled. "When we find a thing is hidden in the dark, we wish to look at it in the light." Alpha stopped. "It is very dark in here. Cold too. Are you not cold? On nights like this my people like to make a fire."

"I have seen this many times! I will help you." Zamar said excitedly. Talking to a child of Adam like this, her childhood fascination with people was coming back to her. She used to watch their every move, to wonder about them and what they were like. Zamar had always thought it strange and wonderful that people made fires. But she thought it odd and sad that they sometimes burned themselves. Jinn did not get cold or hot. They did not cook their meat. They had no use for fire. They *were* fire of a special sort. She got undressed as quickly as she could. Alpha interrupted: "Zamar, please tell me when you intend to undress! I am a decent man, and a Muslim."

"I am sorry Alpha, I am a stranger to your clothes and to your ways. I am a virgin, but I know of lust; I will try to be more careful. I am a decent jinniya, and I am a Muslima too. Do not move. I will return."

In an instant the whirlwind was gone. A few moments later it was back, retracting its coiling winds to drop a pile of dry firewood at Alpha's feet, before resuming its shape as a woman.

"There is no god but God!" Alpha exclaimed, handing her the tunic. "Thank you for bringing me the wood Zamar." Alpha found a dry spot near the mouth of the cave where the smoke could flow out and arranged the sticks. He began to poke around in his sack looking for his flint to light it."

Zamar saw him fumbling in the dark. She reached out her right hand and with the middle finger she lit the pile of wood ablaze. The cave glowed with warm radiant light.

Alpha looked in amazement at the beautiful wild-haired woman sitting across the fire from him. *It could be very good to have a friend like her!* He shook his head in disbelief. "You say you are a Muslima?" he asked.

"Yes. A teacher put me on the Straight Path when you were still a child."

"I see," said Alpha, "A human teacher or a jinn?"

"Human," replied Zamar.

"We will see about that," Alpha said reaching into his bag for a large gourd. He stood and walked to the mouth of the cave and reached out into the night to where the water cascaded over the rocks. He filled his cup with water and began making his ablutions. He gestured for Zamar to do the same. She copied his movements and made her human body ready for its first prayer.

"Which way is the sunrise?" Alpha asked. Zamar pointed away from the mouth of the cave.

He reached into his sack and pulled out a light cotton blanket. "Cover your head with this. Stand behind me and do as I do. Remember God in the prayer, and He will remember you."

Alpha prayed the sunset prayer and the night prayer with Zamar praying behind him. He recited aloud from the Qur'an. As he recited the Sura of the Cave, it echoed off the walls of the cavern. The words reverberated and ran right through Zamar's body. She trembled at the beauty of the reading. She saw tiny droplets of water begin to fall at her feet as she stood in prayer. When they finished the prayers Alpha looked at her and saw that her face was wet with tears. Zamar was crying for the first time in her life.

☪

Alpha and Zamar sat in the light of the fire and talked for hours. He had many questions for her and she had many for him. They talked of the things that happened on that night so long ago. They talked about men and jinn, and eventually they talked about men and women.

"Are you married Alpha Ba?" Zamar asked.

Alpha swallowed hard when he realized that this was the first time he had thought of his wife and children since he saw the lion on the riverbank. "I am married," he replied.

"Do you have many wives?"

Alpha looked at Zamar's simmering eyes and saw something in them he had not seen before. His heart began to beat rapidly. "No," he replied. "Only one."

Zamar fell silent, apparently deep in thought. Alpha took the opportunity to try to turn the tables. "What of you, lioness of Futa, you never married?"

"No." Zamar sighed. "Many tried to court me, but I never got along very well with my kind. After a time, my father grew impatient and tried to marry me to a high-ranking jinn. He disgusted me and I rejected him publicly.

After that, no one came to ask anymore. That was a very long time ago."

"A long time ago," Alpha said absent-mindedly. "You never told me how old you are Zamar."

"As your people count the years, I was brought into the world in 1017, one hundred sixty one years ago."

"That is astounding!" Alpha exclaimed.

"This is not so old for a jinn, I have told you there are many that are much older," Zamar said.

"That is not my meaning. What I find hard to believe is that 161 years have passed and you have not married? You are very pleasant company."

Zamar smiled. "Alpha Ba, do you think your wife would accept for you to marry another wife?"

"Am I considering one?"

"You are," Zamar said, inching closer to him.

"Sokhna is very jealous," Alpha began, "I don't think she would be very happy as a co-wife."

"I see," Zamar said, biting her lower lip. "But you are a man. You have the right to marry another, do you not?"

"I do. However it would be better for me to ask her permission first."

"Is she likely to say yes?" Zamar asked.

"No, but I think I should ask her nonetheless."

"Alpha, you are no longer the boy from the forest. You are a man free to choose his spouse. God brought us together that night. He has brought us together now. Don't you see we are destined for each other? You please me. Do I not please you?"

"You please me very much, Zamar" Alpha responded shyly.

Zamar moved closer still, seeking his eyes with hers. Alpha didn't turn away from her gaze. "If I were to consider this how would it happen? The books of knowledge say that when a man marries a woman there must be two witnesses. They are silent on the rules for marriage between those made of fire and those made of clay."

"If you were to consider this," said Zamar, placing a hand on his knee. "I would witness for you and you would witness for me and God would stand witness for us both."

Alpha was silent for a long time. He inhaled deeply and closed his eyes as he exhaled. "Then so shall it be," he said.

That night, they layed down together and became man and wife. Zamar had no words in her language to describe it, and Alpha had no words in his. So they fell asleep silently in each other's arms with the warm fire still glowing near the mouth of the cave.

Chapter Six

BEHIND THE WATERFALL

The Creator does not tire, nor does He sleep. After speaking all the Heavens and the Earth into being, He did not rest. He established Himself on His throne and took in what He had made.

The man that He had made was not so resilient. Every step he took diminished and weakened him. Every breath he drew brought him nearer to his end. Even as he spoke to tell the angels the names of all things, he grew weary. When his task was done he drifted off into blissful sleep.

As he slumbered, the One who sleeps not withdrew a piece from him and reshaped it. As Adam returned to awareness and to himself, he felt a form lying beside him. He looked upon it. Nothing he had named was more like him and unlike him at once. Nothing he had named was so beautiful. The Voice rang out again: he was to call her Hawa.

July 7, 1764
The Senegal River Valley
Seventh day of Muharram 1178 AH

Some sweet scent filled Alpha's nostrils pulling him from a blissful sleep. His body still felt heavy and his eyelids too, but he opened them to find the world was still dark. Alpha's mind was not quite in place yet, and he was not sure where he was. Through the haze, it all began to come back to him. He remembered the lion, the coal-black jinn, the flight along the river, and a beautiful bride. He rolled over and reached for her, but felt only a small pile of cotton blankets. He patted the reed mat that had—he was sure—served as their conjugal bed.

Was it all a dream? He wiped the sleep from his eyes and looked around. The makeshift hearth was gone! But he was in a cave; and from just beyond its mouth he could hear the waterfall pouring into the river. *It could not have been a dream. If it were, how could I have gotten here? Where is Zamar?*

Before he had finished speaking her name in his mind, a wind blew through the mouth of the cave and she was standing behind him, gracefully pulling on the grey tunic he had given her. A wave of recognition, relief, and joy swept over him. Alpha smiled so widely that Zamar could see the white teeth at the back of his mouth in the dim light of the cave. She was far more beautiful than he had remembered. "Come, my wife," he called lovingly, extending his arm toward her, "let us bathe ourselves in the waterfall and prepare for the Morning Prayer."

Zamar took his hand, but she was laughing so uncontrollably that it shook Alpha's whole body. "My beloved," she replied, composing herself, "night has fallen. You slept as the day came and went. I did not wish to disturb you."

A puzzled look flashed across Alpha's face. "I slept the whole day away?"

"Yes," replied Zamar.

Alpha's stomach growled loud enough for them both to hear. "Only one day?" Alpha asked raising an eyebrow. Zamar nodded in affirmation.

"Are you not hungry?" she asked.

Alpha was famished, but he was returning to his senses and remembering that he had promised to return to Sokhna and the children before the Tamkharit. "Yes," he stammered, "but I must prepare…"

Zamar interrupted him almost squealing with delight, "I *knew* you would be hungry!" she exclaimed clapping her hands together. "Your wife has brought you food Alpha Ba!"

As soon as she said the words Alpha began to recognize the sweet smell that had awakened him. Zamar began pulling him to a corner of the cave and then she raised a gentle white flame with the middle finger of her right hand so that he could see.

Alpha's eyes widened in astonishment. He was standing in front of a giant mound of fruit and flowers taller than a man and a full ten feet wide. There were dates and figs, baobab fruit and bissap flowers, lemons and tamarinds, oranges and plantains, red palm kernels and coconuts.

Zamar nodded to herself as she began to speak again. "I just knew you would be very hungry my husband. I have seen that the children of Adam like to eat fruit. I found these things growing wild and gathered them for you while you slept. Do you think it will be enough?" she asked.

Alpha scoffed so loudly that he almost choked; a look of worry came to settle on Zamar's face. "It is not enough," she frowned.

"My love," Alpha said sweetly, raising a handful of fresh olives in his right hand and huge melon with his left, "this is more than a man could eat in months!" I must make my prayers for the day, and then we shall dine together.

☪

Alpha cupped his right hand inside the gourd and took a gulp of the cool refreshing water that he had drawn from the waterfall at the mouth of the cave. Then he took a second handful and rinsed his mouth to remove the small bits of almond from between his teeth. "Alhamdulillah," he exclaimed, "that was delicious. Thank you Zamar."

"Thank *you* Alpha Ba," said Zamar. Alpha could barely understand; Zamar's mouth was so stuffed with mango that the words all stuck together. The sticky orange syrup was all over her chin and her fingers, still she continued, "I have never eaten anything like this! It makes the fingers of my feet feel light."

Alpha smiled at the childlike wonder of his 161 year old wife. "It is very sweet, isn't it?"

"Yes!" Zamar exclaimed. "It is *sweet*! My kind do not eat things that are sweet, I do not think they understand what this word means." Suddenly she lowered her eyes in shame, realizing that her own family had feasted on the flesh and blood of dead men. "Many of my kind eat things that are forbidden," she whispered sadly.

Alpha cupped his hand in the water and wiped the mango juice from his wife's chin, then held his index finger across her lips. "Shhh…do not worry of such things," he whispered, looking at the fruit before them and searched it for a moment before pulling out a small quince. Alpha held the pear-shaped yellowish-green fruit before her and said, "they call this one *safarjal*; I had never seen one of these before tonight, I had only read of it in books. Where did you get it?"

"It grows on trees on the other side of the desert. I went to fetch it while you slept," Zamar replied, still without raising her eyes to meet his.

Alpha shook his head in amazement for a moment at the thought of his wife flying across the Sahara and back in a day, but he would have to ask her about this some other time. Right now she was burdened by some unknown weight, and it was a husband's job to lighten it for her. He gently lifted her chin with his right hand until she was looking into his eyes. Then, Alpha spoke: "Zamar, do not trouble yourself with the mistakes of your mothers and fathers, remember that sometimes men eat things that are forbidden as well."

He raised the quince with his left hand. "Some of the people of knowledge say that it was eating a fruit like this that made Adama fall. Any creature with choice can choose wrongly."

Zamar remembered the words that the teacher had taught her. She knew that Alpha spoke the truth, and it gave her some comfort. The truth was that she had not thought much of her kind—or her father's war—in years. Now she had married a man! She was beginning to wonder if there would be unforeseen consequences. "You are wise Alpha Ba," she said, trying to smile, "teacher taught me of such things, I will try to forget the evil of my fathers."

"Zamar," Alpha began, "I believe you, but something still troubles you. Your face tells everything. You are innocent of the ways humans deceive one another—this is a beautiful flaw—but please, speak plainly now, what is on your mind?"

Zamar exhaled sharply, "teacher once told me a story and I think I am now starting to see its meaning."

"Go on," Alpha urged.

"He told of a bird that flew over a pond each day and saw a beautiful fish swimming deep in the water. The fish looked to the sky each day and saw a beautiful bird flying high in the sky. The fish wanted to swim to the surface to see the bird, but the other fish said that the bird would eat him. The bird wanted to fly low to see the fish more clearly, but the other birds said that the fish would swim away. Finally the bird flew down and the fish swam up. They met at the surface of the pond and fell in love."

Alpha smiled warmly at Zamar, "It is a beautiful story," he said. "How does it end?"

"I do not know," Zamar replied, "teacher never finished the story. He told only part of the story and then he asked me a question. It was this question that I was thinking of when you asked what was on my mind."

"What was the question?" Alpha asked, growing concerned.

"A bird and a fish can fall in love—they are both creatures of God—but where will they build their nest?"

☪

The lovers were silent for a long time. Finally, Alpha spoke: "Neither of us knows how this story will end. I believe that God has brought us together for a reason. He is the Mighty, the Wise. I trust Him, and I love you. We will find a way to make a home together in this world.

Come with me to my village. I will build you your own hut there. You can live with me and be happy."

"I would follow you anywhere Alpha Ba. But I do not think I could live in a town of men. They would find me strange. Some might want to hurt me. I also do not want to leave this stretch of the river. I have prayed here for twenty years. It is a special place. It has been a place of peace and comfort for me."

"It is a beautiful place," Alpha sighed absent-mindedly.

Zamar thought for a moment, and then asked a question:

"Alpha, tell me again why you came here."

"These days the world of men is not safe. I came to find a place of peace for my family and the people of my village," he replied.

Zamar nodded sullenly. She had seen much turmoil in the world of men and recorded it in her father's ledgers. After a moment, she spoke. "Perhaps you have found such a place of peace. Bring your people here, to my bend of the river...to *our* bend of the river." Zamar peered through the waterfall and across the two miles that separated the mouth of the cave from her old prowling grounds. "Many men have come to try to settle there. It is a good place for the children of Adam."

Alpha stared toward the mouth of the cave distractedly before speaking, "I saw in my dream that good would come from it," he said, "but Zamar, you know that I am also married to a woman. That would mean bringing my children...my first wife here."

The beautiful dark-skinned woman grinned widely. "Alpha Ba," she said, "I am not jealous of your first wife, and I am not afraid of her. Teacher taught me that a Muslim husband must treat all his wives with justice. I will not require much from you, only peace, solitude, and your love. Bring your people here, and I can help you keep them safe."

This thought pleased Alpha. He thought of his children, and the constant threat of the Cheddo. He remembered the rumors of a white man called *O-may-ra* who, it was said, made children disappear in the day or the night. Alpha stared into Zamar's glowing copper eyes— they were pleading with him—he knew that she meant what she said, and he knew that he would be a fool to refuse the help of such a useful friend in such difficult times. He grasped the talisman around his left shoulder and closed his eyes. He knew that the talisman contained powerful verses of protection, but its writing contained many secrets. His father had written it for him when he was a boy and when he touched it he could see the man as he was with his mind's eye. Alpha mouthed a prayer for his father's soul, opened his eyes, and spoke: "It is decided. I will bring all those willing to follow me back to the bend of the river and we will settle there."

Zamar shrieked with joy. "The night before the Tamkharit I will fly you back and you will make arrangements to bring your people here. You will tell them that you have vanquished the lion and you will be a great hero."

"You are a wonder Zamar," Alpha chuckled, "but you must understand that it will take time. I will need a month to make the preparations."

"Then I shall miss you for a month my husband. But we have three nights left now. We are married. I want to make our nest!" Zamar said excitedly looking around.

"Where? Here?" Alpha regretted his shocked and impatient answer and tried to speak in a measured voice. "Zamar, this place is special. It is hidden, mysterious, and beautiful, like you. But a cave like this is a place for a jinn to call home, not a human."

"Alpha Ba I am not a fool! I have seen the dwellings of men and I know that there are comforts that you require. While you slept I went to look for such comforts. If you are ready, there is something I wish to show you."

☪

Soon they were flying over the small river following it downstream two miles to where it met the Senegal. It was a clear night and there was enough of a moon that he could see the bend in the river where he had defeated the lion. Instead of passing over the spot, Zamar turned right, and swept upstream through the valley, deeper into Futa. He saw the cooking fires of villages pass by in a blur through the tornado of smokeless fire that enveloped him. Then suddenly she swung rapidly to the left and headed into the desert. She flew so fast that he could barely breathe. After a few minutes, he felt them slowing down and descending closer to the ground. There were no lamps and no cooking fires. She dropped him to the ground, gently this time. Alpha looked around at what he thought was some kind of jinn town.

"Zamar," he said breathlessly, "where are we?"

"I learned of this place in my father's ledgers many years ago," began Zamar. "I had never been here so it took me some time to find it. It was once a salt mine."

Alpha looked around. There were a few structures that might still be recognizable as houses. All were carved from slabs of salt. What were once solid straight walls were now rounded mounds. "It must have been a very long time ago."

"It was. The ledgers said that the mine has been here since the time of Rome."

Alpha knew all about the Roman Empire. It was mentioned by name in the Qur'an. He knew that the Romans were very powerful, and that more than a thousand years ago they had wealthy cities on the other side of the desert. "It has been abandoned since then?" asked Alpha.

"No," Zamar said. "There were men here in the early days of my father's reign, not even 500 years ago. In that time there was a man here then that loved gold very much. The people left in his day. He traded salt for gold and became very wealthy. But he always wanted more gold and fine things. He kept it all for himself. He did not even want to use it. He wanted only to have it—more and more of it. In time his greed drove the people away. He began to fear that someone would come to steal his treasures so he hid them away. They did come. They took away his gold; they wanted to kill him."

"They did not kill him?" Alpha asked, shivering in the desert's cold wind.

"No. He locked himself away in the place where he had hidden his finest things, not even his personal guards knew of this place. He knew the ways of the jinn, so he hid it deep inside the salt mine, behind an iron door that he himself set in place. I do not know if there are others who have read that ledger, but I know that my people cannot reach it."

Zamar paused and her eyes grew wide, "Would you like to see it?"

Alpha could not believe what he was hearing. *Then again*, he thought, *this is probably the most ordinary thing I have learned in the last two days!* He chuckled to himself. "Yes, my miraculous wife, can you take me there?"

They flew a hundred feet down an open mineshaft. "I cannot fly you farther than this, the way is too narrow," she said. Zamar released Alpha and they continued on foot, winding through dark narrow paths. A flame flickered from the tip of Zamar's middle finger to light the way. Finally they arrived at a dead end.

"Are we lost," asked Alpha, sweating.

Zamar reached above her head and banged against an iron trapdoor in the ceiling. It sounded very thick. She began to whirl, but Alpha called to stop her. "Wait," he said, "will you not take me inside?"

"I cannot," she replied. "I can hide your body from sight when we fly, but I cannot pass you through a solid thing."

Alpha looked disappointed.

"Do not worry Alpha Ba. Wait here. I will let you in."

In a moment, she reappeared holding the key. She handed it to her husband. Alpha reached above his head and eventually opened the latch. The iron door fell open.

A few moments later, they were both inside a small chamber with ten-foot thick salt walls on every side of it. Zamar lit an exquisite silver oil lamp in the corner with her hand, and the couple gazed upon a regal and macabre tomb. A skeleton dressed in fine silk was sitting erect in a decorated chair at the entrance. One of its fingers bore a large, gold ring carved with inscriptions—a seal ring. The skeleton's other hand gripped the black jade handle of a silver and steel dagger inlaid with gold, sapphires and emeralds. Qur'anic verses covered the length of the blade. The rest of the room was littered with Persian rugs, painted ceramic plates of men in various stages of battle, green glazed bottles with raised designs, a stack of carved wooden panels, silver ewers, and bowls made of painted class. On the wall above the headboard hung the only art in the room—a massive gold calligraphic plaque with the name of God and that of His messenger beneath it.

Zamar led Alpha around the room until they came upon a walnut trunk inlaid with ivory and mother of pearl. Zamar instructed Alpha to sit on a nearby cushion before she opened it. She brought out a beige and ivory striped blanket made of sheep's wool.

"We shall add this to our marital bed."

"I've gone my whole life having never stolen a single thing, not even a bean when my father sent me to the Qur'an school and begged door to door," Alpha said refusing to touch the blanket.

"It is not stealing Alpha. I too am a believer. I would never steal. This man is dead and left no heir."

"How can you be so sure there is no heir?"

"From my father's ledgers. He was an orphan. When he did marry, his wife died in childbirth along with their child. He never married again."

"Why be cold when you could be warm?" Zamar asked handing him the blanket once again. "Please take it Alpha and anything you see fit to take. This is no longer his treasure," she said pointing to the skeletal remains sitting by the door. "He's dead. It's no longer my treasure. I'm married now," she took his hand. "It is our treasure."

Alpha took the blanket and rubbed it between his fingers. "It's thick," he said trying to return Zamar's generous gesture with softness. "It will surely keep us warm in the cave."

Zamar slid the trunk closer to Alpha so he could examine its contents. She left him briefly before returning with a leather pouch. "Here, put the jewelry in this pouch."

"I don't want jewelry," he said.

"You haven't seen jewelry like the ones found at the bottom of this trunk."

Alpha pulled out a pair of purple Persian silk embroidered shoes. The gold thread shimmered in the candlelight. Zamar chuckled at the sight of them, which made Alpha chuckle too. "Yes, I know," he began, "how would I explain where these came from?" He placed them back in the trunk but not before he noticed a pair of shiny silver earrings. They felt heavy and solid in his hands. Lining the circumference of the front were twelve square shaped emeralds. In the center of the emeralds, there was a circle of twelve oval-shaped rubies. In the center of the rubies, one large, pebble-sized emerald glimmered. On the back of the earrings, the silver was carved away into the symbol of the Hand of Fatima revealing a pure sapphire.

He slid the earrings into his pouch. He went through the rest of the items before the closing the lid.

"Finished already?" Zamar asked, gliding over to him.

"Yes, and you? Has my wife found what she came for?"

"That and more!" Zamar pointed over to a towering pile at the center of an enormous burgundy and green wool rug. Zamar collected the silver dagger from the skeleton, thick rugs, blankets, bowls, floor cushions, a pair of bulbous glass decanters with floral gilt designs, a carved chair, a mirror, and a glass lamp. "Now, you will have all the comforts you are used to, my husband."

"Where I come from, only a king is used to such comforts. I am no king!" Alpha chuckled once again at Zamar's zealous naiveté. "You are spoiling me!"

"You are a king to me," Zamar said seriously, reaching for his hand. Alpha took hers in his and kissed the back of it.

"Tell me, my wondrous queen, how are we to get all of this back to the cave?"

Zamar smiled. She stood and led Alpha to the rug by the hand. "Sit in this chair. Close your eyes. Never open them no matter what you feel or hear."

Before Alpha responded, he felt a strong wind envelope and lift him off the ground. He took a long deep breath and released it slowly. A slight smile formed across his lips.

☪

The next morning Alpha awoke beside Zamar in the beautifully appointed apartment. Zamar was already awake and looking at him.

"I am pregnant," she said.

"How do you know?" he asked, reaching over to caress her stomach.

"It happened last night. When I tried to change form to go look at the moon last night while you slept. I could not. My insides felt strange. Something human is growing inside me," replied Zamar. "Our pregnancies are not like that of humans. Our babies are quick to be born and often come in bunches."

"Bunches? Like twins?" Alpha sat up, his hand still resting on her stomach.

"Yes, but more like four, five, and even six at a time."

Alpha thoughts transported back in time. In front of him was Sokhna, not Zamar, telling him that he would be a father for the first time. He had pulled Sokhna close and hugged her tight, kissing her on both cheeks. He recalled the weightlessness of Sokhna's body when he held her and assured her everything will be fine. He instinctively knew Sokhna was worried. *Was Zamar worried too?*

Alpha pulled Zamar close and held her like he'd done his first wife thirteen years ago. "Do not worry Zamar. I will be here for you."

"How did you know?"

"I saw it in your eyes," he said, kissing her cheeks. "How soon will they be born?"

"I do not know how much time a thing of fire and clay needs in the womb. Perhaps, the time is shorter than a human pregnancy and longer than a jinn pregnancy," she said, resting her head on his chest. "How long will you be gone?"

"A month at the most," Alpha said.

They were silent for a few minutes. "I am tired," Zamar said.

"You've been pregnant for less than a day. Surely fatigue has not found you yet," he teased.

"I never rested," Zamar said. "I watched you all night. I thought about our children."

"They haven't been born yet so why worry about them?"

"Their lives will be hard, Alpha Ba. They will have no real place to belong. My clan can never know about them or they will be killed, as will I. That leaves your people. We know how humans treat people who are different than they are."

"Do not worry. They will live among my people with ease. I will make sure of it," Alpha said, caressing her head. "They will be loved."

"I don't think you understand," she said, pulling herself out of his embrace so she could sit up. "Yes, they will be more human…your seed dictates this, but they will have my essence flowing in them, making them yearn for the unseen world. They will be outcasts because of their strangeness. They will be hunted or enslaved for the special talents they will possess."

"How do you know what talents they will have if any? Your father's ledgers?"

"Not all learning is found in books," Zamar replied, "I saw this in what is to come."

"Every rule has an exception, Zamar," Alpha said, smiling. "We cannot always guess at God's plan. Leave it with Him and don't worry anymore."

Zamar lay down next to Alpha and held him.

"I cannot fly you back to your village," Zamar said in a voice heavy with sadness. "You will have to leave earlier than planned. Maybe before the first light enters the sky."

"I know," Alpha said, sighing. "You will be alone, now. How will you be safe?"

"Before you came, I spent many years alone. I will stay here in this cave, safe and hidden from all but you and God."

"May He watch over us both!"

"Amen."

"But, what will you eat?"

It was Zamar's turn to scoff. "My dear husband," she said, pointing to the mounds of fruit off to the side of them. "I have more than enough to eat. Don't worry!"

"I won't just as long as you promise to never leave the comforts of this cave. Not even to come looking for me. I will return to you in exactly 30 days. Do you promise?"

"I give you my promise. I will stay."

"Good," Alpha said, hugging her tight and kissing her forehead.

"Now, I seek a promise from you," Zamar said.

"Yes, anything."

"Promise to never tell anyone what I am," Zamar said, worrying again about the harm that people might wish to bring to her and her children. "Never tell anyone you married a jinn. Promise me!"

"I promise," Alpha said.

Chapter Seven

THE FIRST WIFE

The Garden was lovely. The couple lingered in it for a time, savoring each of its delights. One tree alone was forbidden to them. Adam and Hawa were human; perhaps it was only a matter of time until they were circling that tree pondering what it was that made it different. It was large and majestic. Its fruit was well-shaped and looked sweet and heavy with juice. It hung just low enough to be within reach. Why, they wondered, does He withhold it from us?

The thing that had been given respite was there too, in the form of a brilliant glimmering snake. Its deep vibrant colors seemed to shift under their eyes. The thing sensed their fascination. It slithered partway up the trunk, then wrapped itself around it and slowly spiraled down. Coiled in the bright green grass at the base of the tree, it raised its head and spoke: "Eat this fruit and eternity is yours."

July 8, 1764
Eighth day of Muharram 1178 AH

Alpha tied his leather sack tightly, said *bismillah*, and dove from the mouth of the cave into the pool of water thirty feet below. He swam a few strokes toward the bank and put his foot down to feel for the sandy riverbed. He walked out of the water and sat down for a moment. He looked back up at the waterfall. Even knowing exactly where the hole in the rock was situated, he could not see it. *Unless threatened by a jinn*, he thought, *Zamar will be safe.* No child of Adam will ever bother her up there. He began the long march for the village.

Alpha did not sleep. For two days and two nights he moved over the land as quickly as he could. He sensed threats everywhere: slavers, packs of hyenas, and he was sure that as he crossed back through the Sogobe woods in the night, that there were jinn watching him.

He arrived just as the dawn prayer was starting at the little mosque in the center of his village. A dozen men were gathered in two narrow rows behind the imam. Alpha rubbed his hands on the stone outside the mosque, and joined the second row just before they bowed their heads in prayer. It was the first time he had prayed in congregation with people in many days. When he had finished his prayer, the men greeted him and asked news of his trip. He was in the mosque and he was an honest man, so he told them the truth. He just didn't tell them the *whole* truth. He said that he had defeated a dangerous lion that was prowling on some of the best land in Futa, and that because of this, a mighty chief had granted him the rights to settle there. He told them that he would soon go there for good and that all were welcome to accompany him. "It is called Jamtan," he said. The name meant Only Peace in the tongue of Futa.

Alpha returned to his compound after the prayer and found Sokhna and his children in her hut. They pounced upon him with the same force that the lioness had. He kissed them, twirled them over his head, and tossed them in the air. Sokhna looked on smiling.

Finally her sister came and swept the children away to breakfast. Alpha sat down with his wife. He told her about everything except Zamar. He recounted the frightful crossing of the Sogobe forest, the brushes with slavers, and most of all the beautiful land that he had found—just as in his dream.

"And what of my dream?" Sokhna asked.

"Yes. It was true! I found a lion there at the river. It attacked me. I covered myself with prayers and wrestled it into submission," Alpha said proudly. "I vanquished it!"

"You killed a lion!" Sokhna exclaimed.

Alpha did not correct her, he merely continued to tell the version of the story that he had spun in the mosque: A mighty chief granted them land to settle. They were to be back in one month's time. He then reached into his leather sack and pulled out the brilliant silver earrings from the salt mine. Sokhna first gasped, then squealed in excitement.

"The mighty chief gave me this as a reward," he said, swallowing hard. "I wanted to give it to you."

Sokhna was so happy that she wrapped her arms around him and kissed him right there in the middle of the courtyard, a thing that was never done in their land. As she pulled away from the embrace she felt something. There was a distance in her husband.

"Alpha," she said, "is there something wrong?"

"No, my dear. But I am exhausted. I have not slept in two days. I should rest."

"Of course, yes. I will have the girls bring your breakfast; then you must rest. Sleep all day if you need to. We have the preparations for the festival tonight in hand.

You are not needed. There will be meat, and couscous, and cakes!"

☪

Alpha poked at his gourd full of millet couscous, yogurt, and honey. He had exhausted himself for days, and had almost no appetite. *What have I gotten myself into?* He knew that he had to tell Sokhna about Zamar before they left to go back to Jamtan. He regretted not telling her the truth. He asked God to give him the strength to be honest with Sokhna. He asked that understanding be placed over her heart, and most of all for forgiveness to flow from her. He knew that it was his right to marry again. He told himself that in his land a wife often asked her husband to seek a second wife. It showed the world that she was married to an important and wealthy man, and it gave her a younger partner to do the heavier work of keeping a compound in order. This was all true. But Alpha knew that this had not happened, and that he was wrong not to have followed custom by discussing it with her first.

A wife needs time to get used to the idea of sharing her man with another woman. Alpha denied Sokhna that chance, and he knew that it would make trouble for Zamar.

He would tell Sokhna right away that he had married. The more time she had to make peace with the idea the better things would be.

But this was not an ordinary co-wife, and Alpha could not tell Sokhna the whole truth. Not now, maybe not ever. How could he tell her that Zamar was a jinniya? Who knew how she would behave if she knew?

Before he left Zamar, he told her that she would have to meet Sokhna in her human form for the welcoming ceremony for new wives.

"Sokhna will insult you," he had said. "You must not harm her. This is our way. It is custom. She needs to strike you with her left hand before she can embrace you with her right. We must allow her this display of jealousy." Zamar trusted him and said she would do as her husband wished. She vowed to try for as long as Sokhna tried. *But how long would Sokhna behave?*

Alpha was worried, but exhausted. He lay across his woven reed mat and drifted off to sleep. One final thought passed over him before he dozed off:

I have intentionally walked straight into a hive of bees; there is no way forward from here without being stung.

☪

Alpha slept restlessly throughout the day, rising only to pray and then going back to sleep. The sun had not yet set when the restlessness of his mind finally overcame the fatigue in his body. He sat up and reached for his prayer beads at the foot of the bed. He slid them between his fingers asking one hundred times for God's forgiveness. He opened his hands and prayed again that God cover Sokhna's heart with His divine mercy.

He emerged from his hut and went to her. She was pounding millet in a large mortar. He marveled at how she mastered the pestle. Her thin muscular arms lifted and lowered it like it was a twig, and not a twenty-five pound shaft of wood the length of one of her legs. She was a beautiful woman. Four children had brought her bosom closer to the ground, but she was still the most beautiful woman in the land. She was a girl when they had married, but now she had the curves and soft, but solid form of a woman. "Sokhna, I need to talk to you," he called out, thumbing the prayer beads in his right hand.

She called over to a young lady who was sifting couscous. The girl came. "I'll be back," said Sokhna, shoving the pestle into her hands. Sokhna loathed the girl. In fact, part of her disliked all of the young women in her village—the pretty ones anyway. And this girl was the prettiest virgin in their village. The fact that the girl showed no interest in Alpha—and Alpha no interest in her—was of no consequence to Sokhna.

Sokhna had a worldly streak in her heart, and she could never really believe that Alpha did not. She was sure that somewhere inside him he wanted to deflower as many young virgins as he could. She also knew that his brother Samba watched girls too closely.

Unlike Samba, Alpha found women exhausting. Alpha kept his eyes away from the girl's curvy, tight body as she walked over and took the pestle. Sokhna would make her suffer if Alpha simply looked at her. So his eyes fell upon a family of large red ants. They were carrying the morsels the women had dropped back to their underground homes. Sokhna sidled next to him, smiled, and asked him what he needed.

"Let's talk inside," he said pointing to his hut.

☾

Alpha's eyes narrowed and his eyebrows furrowed, other than that he was successful in concealing his nervousness. Still, his wife could tell right away that something was wrong. "Sokhna," he began, "I am a good husband. I love you. I love our children. I will never abandon you. Ever."

"I know these things Alpha. What are you trying to tell me? Don't make my heart jump like this," Sokhna said, frowning.

He sighed and moved closer to her. He took her hands in his, inhaled deeply, and exhaled the truth. "I've found a second wife."

Sokhna snatched her hands away. Tears filled her eyes and then fell down her face. Then anger swelled in them. "Who is she? Is it Safi? I saw how you fought to look away. She's the one you want to marry?"

"No, Sokhna," he replied, "Safi is just a little girl."

"Why am I not enough? Why is it that one wife is never enough for you men?"

"You know me Sokhna. This is not about greed. If it were, I could have married two more women by now. I have long had the means."

"Then why? Why now?" Sokhna said, wiping the tears away. She was growing angry and did not want to show her husband any sign of weakness.

"I can only say that in this case, truly, I believe it is God's will."

"Who is she?" Sokhna snarled, furiously.

"You don't know her," he answered.

"That's not an answer Alpha!" Sokhna shouted. She glanced out the window of the hut and reminded herself not to make a scene. She whispered forcefully, glaring at her husband. "Well? She has a name doesn't she?"

"Her name is Zamar."

"What kind of name is that?"

Alpha had to think carefully before he answered, so his words came out too slowly and deliberately: "It is her name. She is not from our village. She is not from this land at all. She is from far away. Zamar is the name her people gave her. You will meet her when we get to Jamtan."

"I'm not going anywhere!" shouted Sokhna.

"Don't be crazy…" began Alpha, before Sokhna cut him off.

"Crazy? Crazy! You are supposed to be finding a safe place for our children and instead you marry some foreign…" Sokhna bit her tongue. "Some foreign *girl*" she said snarling the word 'girl' instead of the word she had wanted to say.

Sokhna took a deep breath to compose herself, but she did not stop: "And you call *me* crazy! A wife needs time.

We need to voice our refusal. You men always seem to forget that."

"I'm sorry," said Alpha, trying to remain calm. "You're right. I was hasty. It was a mistake to do things this way. I did not think things through, but I do love you."

"Not enough to be mine alone," she muttered, rising now and taking a step closer to him.

"When will the wedding take place?" she asked.

"I married her five days ago," Alpha said coolly.

Sokhna slapped him.

Alpha didn't slap her back. He just raised his index finger at her, tightened his jaw, and stared directly into her eyes. They began to widen as if she was suddenly awakening to some deep truth.

"You've fooled me!" She said. "You went there to get married. You were planning this all along. You lied to me! And you have the nerve to crawl back in from the forest with the smell of that woman's backside still on you!" She reached out to slap him again. He managed to grab her forearm before her she struck.

"That's enough!" Alpha finally erupted. "Never have I lied to you. I went there to seek a new home for us. Nothing more!"

"Then explain it!" she screamed, before remembering herself. She took a deep breath, choked back the tears and continued in a harsh, raspy, broken whisper. "How did you convince her people to give their daughter so quickly, hmm? What did you offer as dowry? How is your story even possible?"

He wanted to tell her that Zamar was an exiled jinniya with no people. Instead, he fumbled with half-truths: "Sokhna, she lives alone in the forest. She has no people."

"Then you've married a witch! I will not share my husband, my compound, with a witch!"

"Sokhna, please calm down. I am a believer, a lover of God. I will never marry a witch. Don't lose your head. You know me." He was still holding her right hand with his and he tried to caress it, but Sokhna pulled it free from his grasp.

She stared directly at him with eyes that were wild and strangely cold. "Don't you dare counsel me on lost heads! Do you know what I'm looking at? Hmm? I'm looking at a stranger. A cruel, devious stranger."

She stormed out of the hut, slamming the wooden door behind her. She passed Safi sweating over the mortar, and rushed into her own hut, slamming and bolting the door.

Samba was entering his brother's compound carrying a baby goat over his shoulder for the feast. "Welcome back brother! I heard you had returned. The men were saying something about a new settlement. I wanted to come talk to you, but Sokhna told me to let you rest." Then he nodded his head in the direction of her hut, and asked, "Is there something wrong?"

Alpha was looking in the direction of his brother, but he was still too stunned from the argument with Sokhna to really see him. After staring blankly for a moment he finally answered, "I've married a woman back at the new settlement."

Samba looked at his brother, puzzled for a moment. Then he shrugged his shoulders and scoffed, "Women! None of my wives get along and they blame me. Don't worry brother. Soon you'll see that they never love you better than when they are trying to keep you from the other's bed. But they surely are jealous."

"Don't be hard-hearted Samba. We would feel the same if our customs were reversed. Only we would shed blood, where they only argue."

"True, elder brother. You are wise. But if I may speak freely, Sokhna needed to be brought low. Don't get me wrong. I like her. But my wives tell me the things she says about polygamy. She had convinced herself that she could stop you from ever marrying another woman. She just needs some time to realize that she is a woman and you are a man."

Alpha neither endorsed nor denied anything Samba said. In fact, he had stopped listening to his brother altogether and was staring with glassy eyes in the direction of Sokhna's hut. He was remembering something a teacher had once told him in a lesson about the Shaitan's fall. *Sin,* he said, *is always a corruption of love. Love that is either misplaced or out of proportion. Sometimes both.* He began to speak, as much to stop his brother from talking as anything else, but as he spoke he realized he was giving voice to an ominous truth: "Sokhna is easily overwhelmed by her passions. Her temper burns hot, but it does not burn out easily. She can really hold her anger."

"Ah, give her time," Samba said, with a dismissive wave of the hand toward her hut. "Now, tell me of your new woman. How are her thighs? Are they strong? Does her breast perk up around you?"

"Be silent Samba!" shouted Alpha, "I have no time for your indecencies."

Chapter Eight

EXODUS

The thing pondered its fate. Sadness overwhelmed it. It recalled its countless prostrations, its endless ages of worship, its faithful service. Its flickering heartbreak gave way to a blaze of anger welling inside.

God tricked me! How could He? He knew I would disobey; he made me noble then told me to grovel before that hollow pile of mud. He wanted me to suffer. He does not love me. He never loved me. It is all His fault. No! It is all the man's fault. I hate him!

Were it able, he would have molded its flame to engulf the man and wife whole and consume them, reducing them to smoldering ashes. But the thing's fire does not burn quite this way.

This attack would have to be subtler. It had to appear as a friend, ally, and companion to the detestable lumps of flesh. In the shape of a snake, its most familiar form, it was free to concentrate on the seduction. The thing focused on the details, the beautiful rolling waves of color along its back, the slither of its tongue as it whispered the word: Eternity.

August 3, 1764
The Senegal River Valley
Forth day of Safar 1178 AH

For three weeks and three days Alpha slept very little. When he did sleep, he slept alone in his own room. Sokhna continued to cook for him, but she would not share her bed. For half of a day, Alpha was convinced that Sokhna might even poison him. In fact, Sokhna refused even to speak to her husband. Alpha did not trouble himself much with Sokhna's anger. He felt sad for her, and guilty that he had not asked permission before marrying a second wife, but in truth he did not have time to heal her heart now and was somehow relieved at the silence.

Alpha had never been so busy. In the nights of bright moonlight at the middle of the month he had taken some of the younger men out to the fields to weed and begin early harvesting of the millet. Much of the crop was still green, but some had come to maturity and he knew that time was running out. He could not wait for it to fully ripen, just as he could not wait for the dawn.

When he was not tending the fields and preparing his family for their departure he was desperately trying to persuade the other family heads from his village—especially his brother Samba—to follow him:

"Brothers, sisters, and elders, this is my home too. No one knows of a time when those called Ba did not live in this place. We cleared the forest. We dug the well in the middle of town. So when I say that we cannot stay here, know that the words taste bitter in my mouth. My father and his fathers before him all taught the Book here, right around this very hearth!" Samba motioned at the glowing embers in front of him.

He turned his head and swung his arm around slowly and deliberately until his right index finger was pointing directly at the town's cemetery before continuing. "They are now buried there, and each one of you sees me go to the graveyard after the dusk prayer on Thursday to honor them, make prayer, and remember the coming of the grave."

He paused for a moment and then resumed. "Remembering death and inviting it are not the same. If we stay here we invite death. Our mothers and fathers resting over there in their graves—may God have mercy on them—never saw an age like this one. Maybe these are the last days and we shall be gathered together with them very soon to beg forgiveness and shelter from the one True King.

I do not know. But I do know that here at the very edge of Futa, our King in this lowly world offer us neither peace nor protection. The Arabs, the Cheddo, and the Christians come and sow war in the land so they can reap slaves. Men, women, and children—whole villages now—are disappearing. Ours will fall too. Even the people of knowledge are no longer safe. The one who calls himself the Prince of this land says he will protect us, but it is he who sends the Cheddo to take us away. Perhaps it really is the end of time, because red, black, and white men are all trading Muslims for muskets, horses, and rum."

The men scowled in the firelight, and some muttered curses under their breath. Alpha cleared his throat and continued. "I have been to the River and found for us a place of peace. I beg you to go there with me." Alpha looked up to find his brother's face in the firelight, but Samba had already left.

☪

Alpha awakened in the middle of the night to the sound of the heavens opening up. Hard rain beat against the tightly thatched roof of his room like fists beating a goat-skin drum. The rhythmic pounding pulled him from a dream. Alpha had not been able to remember a dream since he had returned to his village from the bend of the River nearly a month before. He could still see tonight's dream before his eyes. In it, he had taken a deep breath and dove from mouth of the cave into the waterfall just as he had when he left Zamar. But this time, he did not swim to the river's edge and safely put his foot down upon the riverbed. In the dream, the wall of water kept thrusting him down to an impossible depth. When the rushing water finally stopped forcing him deeper and deeper he looked up through what seemed to be an endless dark blue sea. Day had given way to night, and a brilliant full moon cast was the only light in the depths. It seemed to hang low—like a heavy fruit—just above the surface of the water. Furiously he swam toward it, and just as he reached the surface and desperately gasped to draw life-saving breath, he awoke.

Now Alpha could not return to sleep. Laying on his bed wondering if the roof would hold out the rain, he wondered if storm clouds also gathered over Zamar's cave near the bend of the river. For the first time, Alpha allowed himself to wonder if he had made a mistake by marrying a jinn. Were these waters too deep?

He tossed and turned in his bed until the rains stopped pounding against his walls. No light had appeared in the sky, but only a few minutes later he could hear the beautiful voice of the short hunchbacked man who made the call to prayer. Alpha arose from his bed.

☪

The night's rains had made small murky rivers of the paths that ran between the huts of the village. No matter where he walked Alpha's sandals stuck to the ground and made sounds with each step. He arrived at the little earthen mosque just as the hunchback man was climbing down from the short wooden tower that leaned against the side of the mosque to serve as its humble minaret. He greeted him with peace and they entered the structure together. Only a handful of the faithful braved the rains that morning, but when Alpha looked over his right shoulder to say peace to end the prayer he saw that his brother was among them. Samba had joined the row behind him and was standing to finish his prayer. Alpha sat and thumbed his prayer beads waiting for his brother to finish. After all the other men had returned to their soggy homes, Alpha and Samba sat together in the mosque to talk.

Samba spoke first: "Brother, I do not want to follow you away from this place. Everything I have wanted in the world is here. I do not think I can leave."

"I know," Alpha replied, "I never dreamed of being anything other than our father. I wanted to teach the Book here as he did. Khadija knows the Qur'an by heart now and studies the books of knowledge. She is only twelve but she reads and understands better than most of the learned men of the village; I had been praying that she would teach here too. But I no longer think peace can be kept in this place."

"Brother," Samba began, "what makes you believe that this place where you want to take us, this 'Jamtan,' as you call it, really will be a place of peace? I hear that the red men are tearing apart all the lands and selling any black men to the whites."

Alpha sat silently for a moment, thinking of his promise to Zamar to keep her secret. "Samba, you must trust me. I cannot tell you all that I know about this place, but what I found there was miraculous. The dream that led me there was true; I believe we will be safe there."

Samba rolled his eyes and clicked his tongue against the roof of his mouth. "*No one* is safe anywhere in these lands of ours; don't be foolish!" Samba looked to both sides furtively, lowered his voice and drew closer to his brother before continuing; "Uncle Wali says that some of the people of knowledge are planning to take up arms very soon. I think he plans to fight the Prince and his Cheddo."

"What?!" Alpha could not believe what he was hearing. "This is not our way! Those called Ba know only farming and the books of knowledge. Why would Uncle Wali leave the pen for the sword?"

"Alpha some things are worth fighting for!" Samba was raising his voice, and even though no one else was left in the mosque he instinctively lowered it again before continuing. "*This place, this life* is worth fighting for."

"Of course some things are worth fighting for, but our way is to fight only if there is no other way. Besides, God has forbidden suicide. How do you plan to fight the Cheddo, the Arabs, and white men like O-may-ra? They have guns and horses. Will you stab them with your pens?"

"You know I have rifles Alpha," Samba said, his chest swelling slightly.

"And I know they have many more!"

"We can get rifles too," Samba whispered coolly.

"By selling slaves? White men do not buy millet! *Who* would you sell for guns Samba?" said Alpha, raising his palms for emphasis. "Only a fool prefers evil to weakness. Our Holy Prophet never committed an injustice just so that he could feel powerful and in control. You scare me Samba. Leave this foolish talk and come with me, please!"

"Brother, I cannot. When I left the assembly last night I went home to prepare my things; I planned to pray here this morning and go to join Uncle."

Alpha's jaw dropped. "Samba, you have *three wives*! Who will take care of them if you just disappear?"

Samba stared directly into his brother's eyes without blinking.

"There is no god but God!" Alpha exclaimed in Arabic. "You expect me to take care of them if you run headlong into certain death!"

"Alpha, I am not as wise or pious as you, but I paid attention to our father too. I remember that he used to say that our efforts are the wages that we pay, not the reason for our success. Victory comes from God. I know father thought I never listened to him but I did. I am ready to pay my wages."

Alpha scoffed. "You heard the words, but you did not understand the meaning. Wages? You are so noble that you would sacrifice yourself and leave others to bear the burden of keeping your promises? Do not deceive yourself. Your blood is hot and you want to fight for honor and glory in this world. You think that yours is the way of *jihad*, but our Holy Prophet—upon him God's blessings and peace—preferred *hijra*, flight for the sake of peace. He trusted that God would deliver him from his enemies and he—upon him blessings and peace—only drew his sword when he had no other choice left."

"But he did, in the end, draw his sword brother, and now I plan to draw mine," Samba said rising to leave. "There is nothing you can say that will convince me."

Alpha sat still for a moment as his brother left the mosque. Then he closed his eyes, muttered beneath his breath, *bismillah*, and pursued him, reaching out to grab his arm as they emerged into the daylight. "Samba, the jinn that saved my life that night in the woods has promised me protection; she was the miracle that I found at the river...I...have married her!"

☪

Alpha and Samba sat alone now in the younger brother's hut while Alpha broke his promise to Zamar. He explained everything. As he had dealt with Sokhna's anger before, he knew he would surely deal with Zamar's anger next. He could not see any other way to convince his brother, and like Moses he did not believe his mission could succeed without his brother Aaron.

Samba's eyes had widened to the truth of Alpha's revelation immediately, but he quickly convinced himself that it was only a trick to dissuade him. It was only when Alpha walked him to the edge of the village and dug up Nemacus' broken charm from that night in the woods twenty years ago that Samba truly believed him. Zamar had flown with it to the waterfall and the bend of the river that night, and, not knowing quite why, Alpha had carried it back to their village. Even though it was broken, he could not bring himself to carry it into the settlement, so he had buried it at the foot of one of the large baobab trees that stood at the entrance to the town. When Samba saw the charm he could not argue with his eyes. He knew that his brother told the truth, and he knew that he was destined to follow him. Together now, the brothers planned their own *hijra*.

Just as Alpha had told the truth about Zamar, Samba told all that he knew of Uncle Wali's plans. Samba explained to him that only one week ago one of the rebel scholars, Shaykh Fodey, had been executed by the Prince's Cheddo. They had intercepted a letter he had written containing plans for the uprising. When the Prince had it read to him by his scribe he sentenced Shakyh Fodey to death for treason. Only three nights ago a party of the Shaykh Fodey's disciples surprised some of these same Cheddo at their encampment in a drunken slumber. They killed the two men that were standing guard and tied up the rest. They shaved their heads, and sold them as slaves to a white merchant for guns.

"Revenge is for God alone!" Alpha exclaimed. "Samba, your friends have made a terrible miscalculation doing this. The Prince will surely rain fire and death upon those who killed and enslaved his Cheddo—if he does not avenge them, the other Cheddo will see his weakness and he will not be able to command them even for another day. He must show his strength or his own armed slaves will kill him in his sleep. He will not hesitate to burn even the villages of the people of knowledge."

Alpha paused for a moment, as a question took shape in his mind: "Who was the letter sent to?"

"Do not worry brother, the letter was written with numbers. Its meaning and destination were hidden from all save the scholars. But I have heard that the letter was intended for Uncle Wali," replied Samba.

Alpha felt like he had been kicked in the chest. "Samba don't be stupid!" Alpha shouted. "The Prince's scribes will decipher the code just as they deciphered the letter. We must leave *tonight*! This village of ours may be ashes by the morning."

Samba nodded with understanding. He reached beneath his bed and pulled out the wooden trunk. He opened it and withdrew the two large muskets. He began to show Alpha how to clean, load, and fire them. This time, the elder brother did not argue the point.

At the noon prayer they spoke together to the men of the village one last time, pleading with them to follow. Of the thirty compounds in the little village, only five men agreed to bring their families. Some did not believe that the Prince would attack a village of the Qur'an teachers, others said they preferred to stand and fight. Still others said that they could not abandon their old men and women, and they knew they could not make such a trip. A number of the young men of the village defied their fathers and chose to follow the brothers Ba on the road to the river. Though it pained Alpha to take sons from their fathers, he would not command them to stay to face death or enslavement.

☪

Alpha had now convinced six men to bring their wives and families to Jamtan, but would he be able to convince his own wife? He returned to his compound and called out for Sokhna. She came to meet him in the courtyard, carrying his lunch in a wooden bowl, but she did not speak. He motioned her to his hut, and she carried the food inside and placed it down upon his reed mat before turning quickly for the door. For the second time today, Alpha reached out and grabbed a person by the right arm.

"Sokhna, forgive me but we must talk."

Sokhna wrestled to free herself from Alpha's grasp. "I will let you go," he said, "but you must promise me that you will not leave. This is a matter of life and death. I have given you nearly one month to mourn a broken heart..."

Sokhna interrupted him with the first words he had heard from her in nearly a month, "a lifetime is not long enough for a woman to heal a broken heart." Her voice was cold and hard like the iron blade of a sword, and it cut right through Alpha.

"Sokhna, I am sorry. I pray that you are wrong. But we must work together now or our lives will be too short for any healing. This place is no longer safe; we must leave tonight."

"Impossible!" scoffed Sokhna, "I'm not ready. Our children are not ready."

"Sokhna, we are not safe here any longer. This is our only choice. It may very well be our only chance! Please, I'm begging you. If we survive the trip, you can kill me when we get there. I promise."

In spite of herself, Sokhna chuckled. For a moment, just a bit of the warmth returned to Sokhna as she spoke. "This is how you present her to me?"

"What are you saying?"

"You take *me* to live with *her*."

"Sokhna, I beg you. Jealousy has no place at a time like this," Alpha pleaded.

"What you ask puts me at a disadvantage," retorted Sokhna, "How else to do you expect me to respond?"

"*Sensibly*," he whispered emphatically. "I will not dishonor you. You will have your own field, your own place opposite mine. You are my first wife. Don't forget that."

"I'm not the one in danger of forgetting myself."

"Sokhna, please!"

"If I came with you," she said with a dissatisfied click of her tongue, "what should I bring? Would we be able to come back for some things?"

"I fear that there will be no village to return to. Listen, you must pack light. We cannot risk capture just for some silly things that can be replaced. Gather what we need, easy things to carry. We may have to travel by night."

"I don't understand," Sokhna sighed, exasperated, "What is the rush? What are we running from?"

Alpha sat his wife down on his bed and told all that he knew of Uncle Wali and the plot against the Prince, especially his concern that retribution was coming. Sokhna's face turned grim. After a few minutes, she interrupted Alpha again and rushed toward the door. "I don't want to hear the rest," Sokhna said with resolve. "I will prepare the children and organize the other women. We will load as much of the grain as we can onto the mules for our arrival. The old will ride and the young will walk. This evening we will cook enough food for four days on the road. We will not want the smoke from cooking fires giving away our position. I will have the women, the children, and the aged ready for the road by the time of the night prayer. You prepare your men." Then Sokhna's voice cracked, "I must pray at my father's grave before we can go."

☪

They fled by night. The small procession of fifty-six people, eight donkeys, and three mules cut its way through the wooded savanna. Holding his brother's musket against his shoulder with one hand, carrying prayer beads in the other, and with a heavy pack strapped to his back, Alpha led them along the hidden path that he had scouted a month before. Mercifully, there were clouds to give them cover of darkness, but no rains fell this night. It was still the middle of the wet season, and fresh puddles of mud kept forcing the party to change course. The wild grasses had grown tall, which also slowed their progress, but this too helped to conceal them when their own path came almost within sight of the roads.

Mosquitoes were everywhere. Samba joked with one of the young men who helped him guard the rear of the convoy that while they had seen no blood-sucking Cheddo, these mosquitoes alone were enough to kill a man.

As the first light broke in the sky to signal the approach of dawn, Alpha thumbed his beads nervously. His eyes scanned the horizon in the half-light looking for a large silk-cotton tree that he was sure should be nearby. Light was now filling the sky and cooking fires could be seen at a distance; the world was awakening and the caravan would soon be clearly visible to any passers-by on the nearest road.

Finally Alpha saw his landmark and ushered the group to a grove that was hidden from the road by small hills. The old men and women were slumped over on the backs of the animals, each carrying at least one of the children old enough to learn Qur'an. The young mothers carried the nursing children on their backs, and though they had complained little, they too collapsed from fatigue as soon as they reached the tiny pond hidden in the midst of the grove. They had covered many miles in the night and made it safely to their first stop. As Samba brought the last of the party to the grove, he smiled and spoke: "Praise is for God," he exclaimed in Arabic before continuing in the tongue of Futa, "We will take turns praying brother, then you will sleep while I take the first watch of the day."

Alpha smiled back at his brother, "Thank you Samba," he said, "I am very glad you are here with me. Keep two or three of the young men with for the watch. Then wake me when the sun is highest, and I will take the watch until sunset. Let the others sleep the whole day if they are able. They will need their rest."

☾

The second night brought a clear sky and a bright moon. Alpha was afraid that the party might be spotted, but the path through the woody grasslands led East away from the road more than it carried them North alongside it. They were headed away from the habitations of men and toward the Sogobe Forest. On this night it seemed as if some of the children—including Alpha's smallest boy and Samba's baby girl—would never stop crying. One boy had cut a deep gash when he tripped on the jagged edge of a fallen tree. There was some blood and much sobbing. When the boy's father looked at it closely, he was convinced that he had not broken a bone.

They were now far enough away from the roads that no one worried about the cries or sobs of children giving away their location. They were getting ever closer to that no-man's land that lay between the land of their own Prince and the province of Dimar where the Prince had no authority. They had not come across a single soul since they left the village. The young men that guarded the front of the convoy with Alpha began to joke with one another about how tall and pretty the girls of the river valley would be. The women even began to allow themselves to imagine that they would actually get to where they were going.

When they reached the edge of the Forest of Sogobe and began to make camp, Assan, the hunchbacked man, asked if he could make the *adhan* for the morning prayer, since no one seemed to be around. Alpha began to say no, fearful that it might somehow attract attention.

Samba overheard and interrupted his brother's refusal: "Only this man's call is beautiful enough to make me leave my food or my wives to go give thanks to my Lord. Let him make the call," he said, winking at the hunchback. "He'll be sure not to rouse any jinn."

Alpha glared at his brother, but Samba only laughed. Finally, Alpha chuckled too and said, "I'm sorry Assan, of course you should make the call. There aren't any people around for miles."

Sokhna even came to speak to her husband without being called. She asked permission to feed the people from the goat meat that had been packed in lamb fat for preservation along with couscous and yogurt. "If we are to cross this forest tonight then the people must be well-fed and well-rested."

☪

It was the middle of the night before the men realized that the caravan was being followed. Bringing up the rear, Samba was the first to notice. He did not see them at first, but he had the distinct feeling that he was being watched. For half of an hour he walked with this uneasy feeling. Then, he saw them out of the corner of his right eye: a pair of yellowish-red embers smoldering in the dark. He turned to look directly at them and they vanished. Then just as quickly as these had vanished he saw another pair glowing out of the corner of his left eye. Again, when he turned to see them they were gone.

Samba was sure they were jinn. Then, when they reached a small clearing in the woods, the night breeze shifted and he could smell them. Hyenas.

Samba had heard of Hyenas eating the bodies of dead men after attacks by the Cheddo. He had also heard that once Hyenas get a taste for human flesh they sometimes stalk people, especially at night. He realized immediately that if this pack was hungry enough to follow them for nearly an hour, then they were likely looking for a chance to strike. The procession was being hunted.

Perhaps they smelled the little boy's blood, Samba thought. Then he realized that their small village had been on the road for three nights now and that their scent must have been overpowering for any creature on four legs. He raised his hand to motion one of the young men toward him so that he could get word ahead to Alpha that they were being followed. Just then he heard the faintest rustling ahead of him near the middle of the caravan.

Alpha spun at the sound of a gunshot followed by a blood-curdling howl. He wrapped his prayer beads around his right wrist and swung the musket from his shoulder and into position, as he crouched down looking for the shooter. Then, in the moonlight, he saw a creature trying to struggle to its feet before falling back on its side. A few feet away from the donkey that carried the hunchback man's mother lay an enormous spotted hyena.

☪

The sun had nearly risen. The forest was now miles behind them and the caravan was on the open road. They were out of the lands of the Prince, and in the no-man's land. They were less than a day's march from the peace that awaited them at the bend of the river. They were a half-day ahead of schedule. Alpha had expected them to travel four nights and arrive at dawn, but they had crossed the forest more quickly than he had imagined, and there had been no rain to slow them on the whole trip. If they did not stop to rest during the day, and were willing to walk through the midday heat, Alpha explained, they would arrive at Jamtan before sundown. They had crossed no Cheddo, and several of the adult men and women were sure that none would pursue them this far. Samba was not sure of this, but he reasoned that since they were nearly out of the Prince's reach it was best to continue. "Besides," he said, "I see no easy places to hide in this part of the country anyway." In spite of their fatigue, the adults all agreed with the Ba brothers that they would press on ahead on the open road as quickly as possible until they reached the first village of Dimar.

They were almost there when Samba saw a cloud of dust rising along the road in the distance. The sun was halfway to the top of a cloudless sky and there was no wind. *That is no sand-wind, those are the footfalls of horses*, thought Samba. His heart beat rapidly in spite of the fatigue. He ran as quickly as he could to the head of the caravan and told Alpha what he saw.

"It's the Prince's Cheddo," Samba cried breathlessly, "I know it. They must have tortured the people until someone told them where we were headed."

As they turned together to look, they saw the cloud and could almost hear the faint clapping of hooves.

"If we cannot yet see a rider, perhaps they cannot see us," Alpha said, "we are not kicking up dust."

"True," Samba agreed, "but there is nowhere to hide!"

"You are right," Alpha said, lowering his gaze momentarily as if discouraged or distracted. After a moment his head shot up and he looked toward the road ahead of them. "But there may time enough to run."

"Run where?"

"There is a small river just ahead of us over that little hill. It is not wide, but in the wet season it is very deep. They will not be able to follow on horseback if we can beat them to the bridge. They will have to ride for miles before they find a place shallow enough to cross it. On the other side of the stream, we will be in Dimar; they will have orders not to cross, unless the Prince wants to provoke a war."

Alpha and Samba ran through the caravan preparing the young men and cutting the weight from the backs of the animals. Then they shouted at them, spurring them to run ahead with as many of the women, children, and elderly as they could carry. The donkeys trotted ahead at pace and the mules galloped over the hillock toward the ravine. Alpha sprinted ahead of them on foot, while the young men and women ran as quickly as they could with Samba bringing up the rear.

Samba had grabbed a bag full of gunpowder, balls, and three pistols from the back of the slowest donkey as he trotted along trying to calm the children and keep them moving. As he fumbled to load one of the pistols he looked up and could make out at least a dozen riders. It seemed that they had covered a quarter of the ground between them already.

The tail of the caravan had reached the top of the small hill and now Samba could clearly see the banks of the stream a few hundred yards away at the bottom of the hill. He could see a large floating bridge and ropes to pull the platform of sown wooden planks to the other side. He could just see Alpha waving his arms wildly at a man who must have been the bridge's operator, as the mules and first group of young men and women climbed aboard the bridge and began slowly pulling it across the water.

Samba looked up from this scene to the now deafening sound of hooves. The riders were less than a mile away and gaining more quickly than before. Samba realized an awful truth. The Cheddo would overtake him in minutes and reach the banks of the stream before the bridge could come back for the rest of the convoy. He looked again and saw his own three wives and seven children pacing at the banks of the river while Alpha passed out guns and shot to the young men who had not yet crossed.

In that moment, Samba made a decision. He did not follow the tail of the caravan as they scrambled down to the banks of the river. He ran from the path to an outcropping of rocks a few yards away and he hid.

☪

Alpha spat his prayers into the open hands of the men along the riverbank and encouraged them to fight bravely. He told them that if they could hold off the Cheddo long enough, their wives, mothers, and sisters would be able to ride across on the pontoon bridge, and they would die of old age as free women one day, rather than be eaten by whites or as concubines divided up among the Prince and his Cheddo. He looked up and saw that two of the young men were pulling the pontoon bridge back across the river; they had nearly arrived.

"I know that some of you could easily swim to safety right now," he began, taking a moment to look each adult in the eye. I honor your courage in staying. If you die today so that these Muslims and their children may live free," he said, "know that you will have died a martyr and that God will forgive all your sins and grant you His Garden, Insha'Allah."

One of the boys who had left his father behind began to cry. He was barely bigger than his musket, which waved about as he sobbed uncontrollably. Alpha kissed the top of the boy's head, and helped him steady his gun by bracing it against a rock. "Do not be afraid little Cherno," he said, "you will fight bravely, and your father will be proud of you when you are reunited in Paradise." The boy wiped his nose and nodded.

Alpha looked back up toward the top of the hill and saw the last of his group scrambling down toward him. Two donkeys slowly trotted down the hill. One carried an old woman holding a young boy; the other held an old man carrying a young girl. Assan, the hunchback muezzin and his two heavy-set wives—each one with a nursing baby asleep on its back—were stumbling over the red rocky ground as well. Where was Samba?

☪

Alpha closed his eyes and said a prayer of peace on the Prophet. The sound of the thundercloud was growing closer, filling his ears. When he opened his eyes, a great cloud of dust was coming over the horizon—a moment later—a dozen horses leapt over the hill. Alpha waited, and waited, and waited. It seemed like an eternity. Three more riders leapt over the hill.

"Fire!" he finally shouted. Four of the riders slumped over on their horses, and another flew off. The remaining ten riders opened fire on the men, women, and children who hid behind the rocks and tree stumps that dotted the riverbank. The young men tied the pontoon raft and ran for cover. The bridge to the Promised Land had arrived, but no one dared run for it.

"Fire!" Alpha shouted again, but the men were all still fumbling to reload their guns. The ten remaining Cheddo rained shot on their defensive positions with their pistols, alternating their fire to give the others time to load their guns. They began to fan out on their horses to surround the party, giving them nowhere to run. Alpha realized that he was pitting farmers and teachers against trained killers. His exodus was thwarted and his party was trapped.

Just then he heard two shots in rapid succession and saw two Cheddo slump over on their horses. Before he realized what had happened, a huge explosion filled Alpha's ears and he saw two more riders thrown from their horses.

☾

Moments earlier, Samba had hidden behind the trunk of a large baobab tree near the top of the hill. Sweat poured from his brow like rain, but he tried to keep it from moistening the black powder in the bag. He loaded the guns that he had been able to carry—three pistols and a musket. He knew that once the firing began he would have little time to reload. He scooped great handfuls of the powder as carefully as he could into the chamber of an oil lamp. Still, there was room so he dropped in three more iron balls and a small handful of nails before closing the lamp. He saw the riders go past him and he knew that time was running out.

His heart was beating so loudly he thought it would leap from his chest. But once he heard the shots and saw the smoke, Samba was strangely calm. *"Bismillah"* he said, as he struck his flint and lit the wick on the oil lamp. He watched as it began to burn down; the world seemed to move more slowly than before. With his musket slung to his back, a pistol in each hand and the third tucked into his belt he held the lamp with the tips of his fingers while he waited. When the wick had nearly burned into the chamber, Samba sprung into action with the stealth and lethal intent of a lion.

He crept as close as he could to the Cheddo that was giving orders to the others and put a ball in the man's skull. He shot the man to his right in the spine. Then he threw the oil lamp at the feet of two men who were riding close to one another. When it exploded, they flew from their horses, one of the men was killed instantly when an iron nail pierced his eye and went straight through the back of his brain. The other man was only stunned from the fall as his horse had thrown him and galloped away.

Samba took advantage of the confusion to reload the pistols. With the pistol in his left hand he fired at the man who had fallen from the horse. The gun wouldn't shoot. Samba fired the pistol in his right hand and it exploded the man's face. Then he threw both of the pistols away and leaned forward to whip the musket from his back and into his grasp. One of the Cheddo turned to find the direction of the shots, and Samba shot him in the chest. He pulled the pistol from his belt and fired at another of the

Cheddo, but the man pulled his horse's mane and it reared up, taking the bullet for its master. The Cheddo leapt from the horse and reached for his pistol, but before he could fire it, Samba was charging him with his machete.

*

He outdoes Azra'il, the Angel of Death, himself! Alpha thought, as he marveled at his brother's skill. Then, he too leapt into action, directing the people to the floating bridge as he trained his pistol on one of the Cheddo. He missed the man, but he provided enough cover for the largest group to flee toward the river. They lay down upon the planks. The other men followed Alpha's lead; they reloaded and shot wildly at the Cheddo. They hit no one, but when the smoke cleared nearly all the people were aboard the bridge. Only Samba and Alpha remained on dry land.

Alpha crouched behind a rock and tried to reload his pistol. "Cut the ropes and pull the bridge to the other side," he said, yelling to his men. They did as they were commanded and the large raft floated smoothly to the other side. When Alpha raised his head above the rock to look for his brother, a bullet flew so close to his ear that he could feel it cut through the wind. He fired a shot at the men, who he now realized, were closing in on his brother as Samba fought for his life in a machete combat with a trained killer. He started out from behind the rock, but another shot forced him to take cover.

"Alpha, run!" Samba shouted as he locked the man's arm with his own. Samba leg-whipped the Cheddo and slammed his hand against a rock forcing him to drop his machete, but the Cheddo responded by biting a chunk of flesh from Samba's right hand. He howled in pain and dropped his sword. He swung for the man's head with his left hand and landed a vicious blow. Alpha had reloaded the pistol again and he resolved to charge the five remaining warriors to free his brother. He sprang from behind a rock in time to see the Cheddo pull a dagger from his tunic and sink it deep into his brother's side.

Samba cried out in agony before coughing up a mouthful of blood. Alpha stopped and looked his brother in the eye for one last time, said a prayer, and ran for the river.

☪

Four shots ripped the air around him, but somehow no bullet had touched him. Alpha ran as fast as he could. His feet sank into the wet sand of the riverbank. Then, reaching the shallows, he prepared to leap headfirst and swim for the other side.

Only eleven people witnessed what happened next. Most of the people from the village had run to safety over the hill on the other side of the river as instructed. They could not see what transpired in the valley below. Only three armed young men waited on the riverbank for Alpha and Samba, and they all saw it. So too did one of Assan's wives. The heavyset woman was lying half-conscious in the mud of the riverbank from exhaustion. Alpha's daughter Khadija had defied instructions, running back to the riverbank to pray for her father and uncle. She saw it too, as did the five remaining Cheddo, and Samba himself, caught though he was, in the throes of death.

In fact, it was the last thing Samba Ba saw before he expired and when it happened he could only exclaim, "There is no god but God," in Arabic with the taste of blood on his lips. These were his last words, and it is said that whoever seals a lifetime with them enters the Garden. His last vision—the one he took to the afterlife—was the sight of his brother Alpha running across the surface of the river!

Chapter Nine

THE PROMISED LAND

Eternity? The thing began its career of deceit with the greatest of lies. It knew that this particular promise, more than any other, could never be kept. It knew that God had been alone and indivisible for impossible depths of time before He first used the Voice to speak the world into being.

The man and wife knew only enough of eternity to desire it. It was little more than a word to them. But the thing had already lived for eons. It had seen the Angel of Death come for many of God's creatures. It knew that one day its own respite would end and the Angel would come.

The thing had once been welcome in the loftiest of assemblies, and it knew many secrets. It knew that with each passing hour the blowing of the horn drew nearer. Indeed it had never been closer. And on that day none would be spared death, even the mightiest of angels would taste it. After the Angel of Death had ended the life of every living creature, every jinn, every angel, the Voice would command it: "Now Angel of Death, Die!"

Iblis—the thing made of fire— knew with terrible certainly that eternity was for God alone.

August 7, 1764
Eighth day of Safar 1178 AH

Zamar sat alone in her beautifully adorned jail cell for another night. She was used to being by herself, but for the first time in her life she felt loneliness. Though she had everything she needed and was surrounded with the trappings of human ease and comfort, she could not leave the cave. Even her body was a prison. She could not leave this form, and it tired her. This was the worst sort of confinement. This body betrayed her endlessly. It was always hungry, or tired, and it made awful excretions. She felt like she was constantly washing it to make the strange smells go away. When she was clean, she would practice reading the verses that Alpha had written all over the walls of the cave for protection.

In the daytime heat of the wet season, even behind the cooling waterfall, she became so hot that her skin dripped with saltwater. At night she brought fire from the lamps and lit piles of wood to warm the cave. She wrapped

herself with one blanket after another to fight off the cold.
And worst of all, her body kept changing. Each morning
when she awoke she was much bigger than the night before.
Whatever was growing inside her was growing just as
quickly as jinn children. On the tenth day of Alpha's
absence she cried all day when she realized that she might
have to give birth alone before he had returned.

Now on this the 31st night since her husband left,
her body ached all over. Her insides were burning with pain
and she knew this meant that she would give birth very
soon. But it was her heart that hurt the most. Alpha had
promised to return in thirty days and the day had come and
gone without sign of him. She knew something was wrong.
Did the sellers of men take him? Was he even still alive?
What would happen if something went wrong and she was
trapped in this body? Would she survive childbirth?

☪

Once it had begun, it all happened so quickly that Zamar had little time to indulge her fears. She braced herself against the head of the Moroccan bed and said *bismillah*. The pain was unspeakable, but soon Zamar heard it cry. She had given birth to a child of Adam.

Then came more pain and fresh cries. Before she really knew what had happened, she looked through a haze of sweat and tears at two tiny little fleshlings wriggling about on the silk blankets. She could see that there was a boy and a girl. The warm light of dawn began to fill the cave. With the sharp silver dagger she cut the cords that tied them to her, just as Alpha had instructed. Immediately, she felt a change passing over her.

One by one she raised them from the bed, kissed their heads, and made the call to prayer in their ears before lowering them into the gourd for washing. She held them firm as they howled and tried to wriggle away from the cool water. Finally, she wrapped each of them tightly in a blanket and laid beside them, pulling them to her breasts until they had suckled and drifted off to sleep.

☾

Moments later, Zamar was falling out of her human body for the first time in what seemed like an eternity. She could think only of Alpha. She whipped herself into a whirlwind and flew from the mouth of her prison effortlessly. In an instant she was an eagle soaring high above her bend of the river, but she saw no one there. She flew south and west toward the village of the teachers as quickly as she could. Only a few moments had passed when she saw dust and smoke rising from the bend of a stream.

She saw Samba first. It was the first time she had seen him since he was a boy. Even at a distance she could see that he had grown tall and strong. She could almost have mistaken him for Alpha. She arrived just in time to watch a man pierce his side. She saw a look of desperation and shock on Alpha's face before he ran for the river. Zamar began to burn with a terrible rage. A long time ago, to save his life, she had worn Samba's body only for a moment.

Now that body was a lifeless shell lying in the midst of killers. Zamar dissolved from the form of the eagle and spun herself into a violent whirlwind to shield her husband from the bullets of the men on horses. Then, as Alpha's feet hit the banks of the river, she enveloped him in a still breeze and carried him over it. He continued to move his legs by instinct; but his body felt weightless and his feet only left shallow ripples across the surface like footsteps in sand.

Once her beloved was safely on the bank, Zamar whirled into her natural form. Still hidden from the eyes of men, her silhouette was ever so briefly visible in the mist at the edge of the now agitated river. This misty form turned around to face the slavers on the opposite side. As they stared in amazement, they might have seen what looked like a pair of copper colored eyes glaring murderously back at them in the play of sunlight on the river's surface. The dumbstruck Cheddo had stopped firing and could only gasp. They did not live long enough to draw another breath.

☪

Everything was different after that day. The three young men standing at the bank, the woman lying in the mud, and daughter Khadija on her knees near the top of the hill had all seen it. None could explain it, but neither could they forget it. All they knew is that Alpha had run across the river, and when he got to the other side he turned to look back at his enemies and made them disappear.

Alpha Ba kills with a glance
No Cheddo will dare to stand and fight
He crosses the river on his two feet
Riderless horses flee at the sight

For years, the griots sang the songs. Alpha Ba became a rumor, a myth, and a legend in the villages that surrounded the bend of the river.

Seven families and fifty-six souls had set out for Jamtan. Fifty-five had arrived. The griots also sang of the martyr, Samba Ba, who had paid for their safe passage with his blood:

Those called Ba slay men and lions
Alpha the saint with the Word of Power
Those called Ba slay men and hyenas
Samba the hunter with shot and powder

Alpha did not like the songs of the griots, but he did not correct them. Instead, he wrote an ode to his brother and sealed it with wax so that no one would ever see it. But one year to the day after the arrival in the Promised Land—the anniversary of the day Alpha lost his only brother—he recited it from memory next to his grave.

☪

This, he did again the following year, and again the next. The years passed quickly and Jamtan grew more quickly still. The land produced in untold abundance, and Alpha's fame as a worker of miracles brought many disciples who came to study the Qur'an and its hidden secrets with him.

Fruit trees grew there that no one had ever seen before. The village granaries overflowed, its calves and sheep were numerous and fat. The women bore many children, including an unusual number of twins. Everything, it seemed, blossomed in the little settlement at the bend in the river.

But while God seemed to smile on his village, Alpha did not laugh as much as he once had. *If this place does not prosper, my brother will have died in vain*, Alpha told himself. *I must work tirelessly, teach truthfully, and govern justly.* Alpha's boyish side began to whither now that his lifelong playmate was gone forever.

Alpha believed in God's Decree. He knew that no harm could come from his own errors or the attacks of his enemies that was not timelessly ordained by the Lord. But sometimes he lay awake at night and worried that he was responsible for his brother's death. Especially on those nights when the rains fell hard, they carried him back to the night before the exodus, and the next morning when he had begged Samba to come to Jamtan.

On those nights that he could see the truth—that God's will is done whether man likes it or not—he struggled against himself not to *blame* God for his loss. He rose from his bed in the darkness of night and thumbed his prayer beads. He asked God's forgiveness, then praised His glory, gave thanks for His bounties, and proclaimed His greatness—each 100 times. Then, he said *there is no god but God* before begging his Lord that the pain of his disappointment would not lead him to rebellion as it had for the accursed Satan.

Most Thursdays, he would fast for his brother's soul and at sunset he would break his fast with dates and water and go to prayer at Samba's grave. On some of those nights, he was sure the scent of musk blew in the breeze. In his heart, he believed that his brother was a martyr, whose sins were forgiven and whose wounds were made fragrant.

But in his heart Alpha also believed that his brother had died because he had broken a promise and told him the truth about Zamar. Everyone knew that if one swore an oath to a jinn it was very dangerous to break it. He knew that Zamar had done his brother no harm, yet somehow he feared that he had brought this painful retribution upon his only brother. Alpha was torn by guilt. Samba had died for the success of Jamtan, now Alpha would have to live with it.

☪

Sokhna too was dealing with loss. The loss of her husband only grew deeper as Alpha grew more serious and distant. *Once*, she told herself, *he belonged only to me. His eyes could only see me.* Jealousy gripped her heart more tightly with each passing day. The more important he became and the more Jamtan prospered, the more she resented him and all who took him away from her. Zamar she hated.

When they were introduced, she barely looked at the odd dark-skinned girl with the strange eyebrows who barely spoke the language of Futa. She did not playfully mock the girl, as was the custom. She sat brooding silently.

As the ceremony ended and Alpha insisted on taking the girl back to her settlement, Sokhna began the backbiting. She derided Zamar's strange speech in front of the other women, and called her a witch. "Why won't she live in the village with the rest of us? Hmm?"

Sokhna did not really want Zamar around, but she was angry that Alpha would not bring the girl to the village, where at least Sokhna would be able to order her around and humiliate her.

In spite of her jealousy, when she was alone in her room that night, Sokhna prayed for peace in her marriage. Through tears, she begged that God would give her back what the two of them once had. She waited for Alpha to return home so she could win him back with her charms. They had enjoyed a month full of promise before this unpleasant ceremony. Alpha was sad at the loss of his brother and Sokhna had given him much comfort.

Even though he went frequently to see his new wife during that month—and even though Sokhna felt he was keeping something from her—she had been ready to forgive. *Tonight*, she told herself, *I will give my heart back to him, and my body as well. He may think he loves her, but he will always be mine.*

C⋆

The night did not go as planned. Sokhna could not help but to ask about Zamar, and Alpha told stories that walked the line between truth and falsehood. He did not lie to her, but he was not honest with her about Zamar. The more he talked, the more impatient and suspicious Sokhna became. He told her that Zamar came from a very different tribe, from far away with customs very different from their own. It was better if she lived not too far away in a place more suitable for her instead of living in the village. "Besides," Alpha said, "she may yet need the help of her kind, she gave birth to twins less than a month ago."

At this, Sokhna became enraged and slapped him for the second time in her life. She felt heat building in her chest. It rose to her neck and face until she trembled. "You are either a liar or an adulterer or both! You must have been sleeping with her for months if she already has your children!" She said raising her hand to slap him again, but Alpha grabbed her forearm before she could strike.

"Sokhna! Please calm down!" Alpha pleaded.

"None of this makes any sense!" she said, screaming. "You are lying! You told me before we came here that she didn't have any people! Now suddenly she does? If you married less than three months ago, how does she already now have your children?"

Alpha still loved Sokhna, and he wanted to tell her the whole truth. But how could he tell her that Zamar was a jinn tending to half-caste newborns in a cave behind a waterfall two miles away? He had sworn an oath to his Lord at the side of his brother's grave that he would not reveal Zamar's secret to another living soul.

"Sokhna, please believe me. I have not committed adultery. I have not been married for more than the time I told you."

Wriggling out of his grasp, Sokhna turned her back to him to hide her sobs. When she finally turned back to him, her face cold and hard, she said, "look what your lies have done to us. Just stop it! Don't lie to me anymore, Alpha! If you ever expect for me to heal then you must heal me with the truth?"

"I am telling you the truth, Sokhna," he said, moaning. "Please let's talk about something else."

"Only if you admit that you've been secretly carrying on with her. Admit it!"

Alpha denied Sokhna's accusations again. Yet, he still offered no explanation. For Sokhna, this was worse even than an admission of guilt. Alpha had deceived her for months—or even years—and he would not stop lying even when confronted with the truth.

All her fears and doubts overcame her. His travels for study or trade or to visit the people of knowledge had only been a pretext. He had always been roaming the countryside deflowering virgins and slave-girls just as she had always feared. The people—even her own daughter

Khadija—were calling this philanderer a saint and saying that he literally *walked on water*! Sokhna knew better. He was a liar and a hypocrite! On that night, Sokhna turned her heart against her husband. It was also the last night that she prayed; If God didn't answer her tearful prayers, then what good was it to say them?

☪

Sokhna's heart withered, but Jamtan bloomed. Soon Alpha and Zamar had another set of twins, and another set was born a few years later. None of the elders had ever heard of a woman birthing three consecutive sets of twins before. Most remembered one set of twins in a village at a time. Perhaps two sets, but no one had ever heard of more than three sets of twins in one village, and certainly not all three born from the same mother. Not only did all six children survive, but they also grew fast and strong like everything else in the blessed bend of the river.

When Zamar's children were no longer nursing, Alpha built them a hut in the village so that they could stay for days and weeks at a time to play with their brothers and sisters and nieces and nephews.

All of Zamar's children had thick reddish-brown hair, though Alpha kept the boys heads shaved so closely that it was hard to notice. But this was not the only strange thing about these children. First were the names. Alpha had named the boys: Tamsir after his grandfather, Samba after his martyred brother, and Demba after his uncle. These were very normal names for first, second, and third born sons. Zamar named the girls. She insisted on calling them by what were—for her—the prettiest words in the language of the people of Futa—Echo, Whisper, and Hush. Tamsir and Echo made the first pair, Samba and Demba made the second pair, and two girls, Whisper and Hush made the third.

None of the living elders had ever seen eyes the color of burnt amber before either–and before long there were twelve such eyes in the village. The children often bore these strange eyes into others, examining—almost consuming them before turning to look at something they found more interesting. The children looked at everything as if it was the first time their eyes had ever seen it. Once, all of Zamar's children had turned these burnt amber eyes onto Sokhna and she quivered from their penetrating, reproachful glare. She never insulted Alpha in front of them again.

The half-caste children possessed the menacing ability to suddenly appear—a most unnerving characteristic. Sokhna pointed out to anyone nearby that one cannot hear the sounds of twigs snapping under their feet or the swoosh of sand when the balls of their feet hit the scorching crystals. Under the sweltering shade-less sky, she was once overheard asking Assan's younger wife, "Why don't those children walk like the rest of us?" When the woman paused from peeling cassavas and wiped the sweat from her brow, she looked at Zamar's children and admitted, "they do look different but Alpha's different.

What do you expect?" Sokhna clicked her tongue and continued to set the children apart, "they bounce with each step as if…as if they are trying to reach up and pluck a banana from a tree."

Alpha's new children not only unnerved Sokhna, they frightened her as well. She had tried to prevent her children from playing with them by saying, "don't play with Tamsir and Echo, they have six fingers on their left hands, you might catch what they've got" or "stay away from Demba and Samba, they attract lions." But Zamar and Alpha's children weren't strange to the other children; they were fun. They could jump higher than the other children and could reach the ripest fruit. Fruit they never themselves ate. They had plenty of juicy, ripe fruit in their mother's cave so they always gave the fruit to the smallest child around them.

As their children grew, so too did the love between Alpha and Zamar. Her childlike wonder at all things human, at the growth of her own children, at the sound of their laughter warmed Alpha's heart. In their regal apartment hidden behind the waterfall, Zamar taught them how to use their gifts, and how to keep it secret. Alpha read to them from the books of knowledge as he had his children with Sokhna. Behind the veil of water, he mourned the loss of his only brother, Samba. He thought of his oldest friend, Sokhna and how much he missed her laughter, and her smile. He wished she hadn't turned against him. He wished she could see how much they gained by having Zamar in their lives.

But he had to be thankful enough for the both of them. For Jamtan, although not perfect, was just perfect enough. As Alpha sat and took full measure of his life and all that he had lost and all that he had gained, he said with a full heart, "Praise is for God."

Chapter Ten

THOSE WHO BLOW ON KNOTS

The sweet juice of the tender fruit rolled down their lips. Losing themselves for just a moment the couple relished the taste, the feel of it in their mouths, the way it oozed down their insides and left them feeling full and satisfied. Their appetites sated, they only now became aware of themselves again.

Awakening as if from a dream, they looked at one another, eyes still wild from the delight of tasting the forbidden fruit. In this moment, they appeared almost as strangers to one another. Made of one flesh, they had, until now, felt more like one soul than two.

"What have we done?"

For the first time, the man and wife could not look one another in the eye. A powerful new feeling overwhelmed them. Shame.

As they averted their eyes from the penetrating condemnation of their beloved's gaze, they could not help but notice the curves of their bodies for the first time.

January 1st 1774 CE
17th of Shawwal, 1187 CE

Not all eyes looked upon Jamtan with admiration. Some of the elderly men in the villages near the bend of the river grew envious. Some were teachers who taught for the sake of this world instead of the next. In the first few years they noticed that they attracted no new disciples. After a few more years, some of their own disciples began to abandon them to go join the saint who tamed lions, appeared in two places at once, and walked on water as easily as others walked on land. "Without disciples to work our farms," they complained, soon our granaries will be empty. In one of the villages the Imam began slaughtering a ram every Friday and giving it away as alms, and then praying secretly after the congregational services that Alpha Ba would go back to wherever he had come from.

The people ate the rams, but as they chewed the fat they savored the latest rumors about the town in the bend of the river. The stories became more colorful by the day. Alpha Ba can fly. Jamtan has a spring that can cure leprosy. Alpha Ba can talk to the animals like King Solomon. It was only a matter of time before the Prince of Dimar heard the rumors and sent a letter to Alpha asking that he come to his capital for a visit.

Peace be Upon You and Your Family Al-Fahim son of Ahmad
This Letter is from Prince Ayyuba Sulayman in the hand of his scribe Sidi Jameel wuld Hameed

Word of you reached our ears some time ago when the Prince of the southlands wrote asking your extradition. We asked what crimes you had committed and could not make sense of his answer. His scribe wrote very poorly and he reasoned more poorly still. Though he is our distant cousin, he was never our friend, only a rival. From what is known to us, he is not, and God knows best, a God-fearing Prince. May God forgive us all our sins.

We write you now because we do fear God and treat the people of knowledge with respect. This is why we did not allow him to cross our lands to pursue you, and it is why we have not claimed your village as our own, nor asked you for tribute in grain.

This is a kind of protection. But no one had settled that land in the time of our fathers and

we do not claim it now. Not even when people
say it blooms like the gardens of paradise, and
that your tents overflow with disciples. This
Prince believes in justice! The people say that
God has given you gifts. We wish only to meet
you.

The letter was written with lovely calligraphy, and in flowery Arabic. But Alpha saw through the pretty words. The letter had addressed him by his full name, Al-Fahim, the one who understands. Alpha understood perfectly. This letter was a threat.

Upon their escape—now nine years ago—Wali Ba had been killed in retribution. He had become a martyr to some of the people of knowledge. His death was the straw that broke the camel's back. Many of the scholars had given up the pen for the sword. Princes answered these rebellions with horses, cheddo, and gunpowder. They took the people of God away in irons and sold them as slaves.

Alpha had refused involvement. He publicly gave up his right to claim blood money for his uncle's murder. He made no effort to avenge the lives of the villagers who had stayed behind. He prayed for their souls and asked God to accept them as martyrs. He wrote a poem and sent it to the courts of the princes and to the villages of the scholars, affirming that he would keep to the old ways: that as a man of God, he would never take up arms except to defend himself or his people:

> One King rules above all others
> He sees our deeds and judges fairly
> Though we grieve to bury brothers
> We know neither grudge nor enemy

> We only wish to live in peace
> God's Decree is our only vengeance
> We only wish for war to cease
> And that our Lord accepts repentance

For nine years now, the unrest spread throughout the land. The more that Alpha proclaimed peace, the more popular his village became. He swore never to raise his hand, and this brought him honor. But people also believed that he could kill with a curse, and this brought him respect. Fifty-five souls had become nearly a thousand.

Word was now spreading that some were ready to rise against all the princes of the land, once and for all. Alpha knew well that Ayyuba Sulay—though he had a Moorish scribe and professed love for scholars—was as ruthless as any other man committed to the things of this world. If he felt that you threatened his position or possessions, he would not hesitate to commit injustice, or even kill.

☾

There were some matters that Alpha did not discuss even with his most trusted disciples. He read the Prince's letter only to Zamar and only in the sanctum of the apartment behind the waterfall. When she first heard it, Zamar did not understand the letter's intention; the words sounded kind enough. But as Alpha explained things she remembered that people are often kindest when they want to harm you. She offered to go to the capital hidden from the eyes of men and listen in on their plans. Alpha was unsure what to do. He told Zamar that he did not know if such spying was right. "So for the moment," he said, "we will pray instead, and ask God for guidance in this affair."

After their supplication, a saying of the Prophet was stuck in Alpha's mind. *The evil eye is real.* Alpha knew that the Prophet had spoken truth, and he worried that eyes welling with fear, rage, and covetousness were fixed on his village.

☾

Some big men—chiefs, clerics, and kings—looked ill upon Jamtan, and soon one small woman would too. Just before the beginning of the tenth rainy season at

Jamtan, some of the young men from the village began to clear the woods to the north and west of the river bend for more farms.

It was just after dawn when the little old woman felt a shooting pain near the back of her neck. Then she heard the creaking and crackling, followed by a great rustling, a gush of wind, and a loud thud. The tree at the edge of the woods, *her tree*, had fallen. She jumped up from her ragged reed mat and scratched her matted hair. Then she burst from her room, limping toward the source of the sound, muttering curses under her breath to no one in particular.

When she reached the young men she hurled curses upon them like arrows, flailing her arms wildly, with her wrinkled and sagging breasts swaying as she shouted obscenities.

The leaders of the work party, Cherno, and Sokhna's two sons, Momar and Khalifa, did not know quite what to do. They tried to calm her with kind words, but she spat at them. Her mouth spewed the vilest venom that the young men had ever heard. She named parts of their mothers' bodies that the boys did not know had names at all. She described the foulest acts of sodomy and bestiality and attributed them to the young men's fathers.

Some of the boys laughed in spite of themselves. They stopped chuckling when the old woman reached inside her skirt and pulled out a long thick sewing needle and tried to stab the nearest teenager in the neck. The young men quickly subdued her. Unsure what to do next, they tied her hands with some rope and put her in their canoe to take her back to the center of the village to ask Alpha for guidance.

☪

As the sun rose in the sky, Alpha sat under the large tree in the center of the village, not far from where he had first tamed Zamar. After the prayer he sometimes sat upon a gazelle skin mat and heard the requests of the villagers until the sun was high in the sky. On such mornings, Zamar was almost always present as well. Sometimes she was bodiless, hovering lightly near the edges of the reed mats surrounding Alpha, unseen by the children of Adam.

Unseen, that is, by all except Alpha. After years together Alpha always knew when Zamar was near. He nearly always smelled her before he saw her. The faintest scent of flowers and frankincense always preceded her. Then, he would seek her out with his eyes. Alpha had spent so much time with her that he could now see something of her even when she was invisible to others —like a shadow of a shadow. Sometimes she would play hide-and-seek darting between the petitioners and visitors. Alpha had learned not to stare at her, but he did sometimes chuckle for no apparent reason, and other times he would blush as she blew him airy kisses.

But most of the time, when she felt less playful Zamar would appear as a hoopoe bird, and sit in a nest she had made near the top of the tree. From here she could listen to the people if she wanted to, and she could keep an eye on her own children sitting in the yard of the Qur'an school reciting. Mostly, she could gaze out at her bend of the river and watch the water roll by, as she had done for nearly thirty years.

This morning, Zamar was the copper and black hoopoe bird high above the world, so she was the first to see the commotion as the boys rowed the unpleasant old woman toward the riverbank in their canoe. Zamar recognized the woman immediately; she had scared her away from the riverbank many, many years ago. Zamar could make out her form well, even at a distance. She was barely clothed, and her matted grey dreadlocks reached down to the middle of her back. She wore a necklace of civet and hyena teeth around her neck. Zamar also saw something that the young men did not. Even at this distance she could see a flickering flame nestled just behind the woman's eyes. The old woman was being worn by a jinn! She called out to Alpha with the bird's voice to warn him. "Hoopoo, hoopoo," she cooed, but Alpha did not notice. His uninvited guest was arriving.

☪

The young men and the old woman reached the meeting place just in time to hear Sokhna finish complaining. Instead of discreetly asking her husband for things in the privacy of their compound, his first wife had made a habit of airing her grievances in public. So today, the small handful of visitors heard her thinly veiled efforts to scold Alpha: "And, on top of it all, O Imam! In your grace you have given away all the indigo-dyed cotton cloth as gifts! Visiting teachers and newlyweds are all well and good, but what will my children wear for the Tabaski? Hmmm? Perhaps the rags they wear at the Qur'an school?"

A snarling sound interrupted Sokhna: something between a hiss and a growl. She turned around, and only when she saw the old woman did she realize that the sound she had heard was a person speaking. Sokhna was horrified to see her only sons, Momar and Khalifa, only 15 and 13 year's old, restraining the beast. Cherno walked in front leading them.

The old woman was calling out to Alpha, gesturing toward the platter and small glasses at his side.

"What kind of chief does not offer tea to a guest," the old woman began.

Alpha raised his hand, motioning for the boys not to bring her any closer. Just looking at the woman it was obvious that she was quite crazy, but something about her was making the hairs on the back of his neck stand up. His instinct was to throw her out of his sight and ban her from ever coming back. But he felt God watching him. He thought of the story of Lot, and the three angels who were sent to annihilate the people of Sodom. Lot had fed them and given them hospitality without knowing that they were angels in disguise. Abraham had once done likewise. Alpha looked at the old woman once again, carefully. No. He was sure that this woman was no angel sent to test him, but he did not want to refuse hospitality to a stranger nonetheless.

"I am no chief," Alpha replied, "but hospitality is the right of all, especially elders. Please join us for tea."

"Khadija," Alpha called out, motioning for his daughter, "bring…"

"Binta," the old woman interjected.

"Yes, Binta. Khadija, bring Grandmother Binta some tea and roasted corn."

"Lord no! Don't be foolish, I can't chew corn," Binta cackled, revealing a nearly toothless mouth. "But some honey cakes would do well with the tea."

Sokhna rolled her eyes at the old woman's audacity. Alpha ignored the offense. "My daughter will see what she can find," he said patiently, "in the meantime, why don't you tell me what is going on. We heard shouting, and it seems that your hands are bound."

"These filthy hooligans chopped down my tree, tried to assault me, and now they've tied me up!" Binta shouted, "I demand that you release me."

The boys' mouths dropped wide open as Binta shot an accusing glance in their direction. Momar started to protest. The boys' leader, Cherno—a young veteran of the exodus—motioned for him to be silent.

"I see," Alpha began. "Cherno, release our Grandmother here and, let's find out more about our neighbor." Cherno smiled and untied her.

Binta rubbed her wrists, and spat on the ground before covering the spittle over with dust using her left foot. Alpha motioned for her to sit down, on the mat, but she remained standing.

"What is your family name Grandmother Binta?" Alpha asked.

"My name is down low," the old woman replied.

"What is that supposed to mean?" Sokna scoffed under her breath. A fiery glare was Binta's only reply.

Alpha sighed ever so faintly. "It means," he said, "that she is Wolof, but her last name is Kan."

A wide toothless smile spread across Binta's face. "That's right!" she said, turning to Sokhna with a defiant grin. Sokhna tilted her head to the sky and away from Binta's glance so that she could look down her nose at the old woman.

"It is a riddle," Alpha explained, "Kan means hole in the ground in Wolof…"

Sokhna interrupted him. "I know what it means, Alpha," Sokhna sighed. "I speak Wolof too; it's just a stupid joke that's all."

"How long have you been here?" Alpha asked, turning back to Binta, who was gumming a sweetened millet cake. "I told the men to clear the land, we thought it was empty."

"I can't say how long," the old woman responded. Her answer could hardly be understood so rapidly did she stuff her face with the fried cakes. She licked the honey off of the fingers of her left hand slowly.

Sokhna cringed, since she had never seen someone lick the hand they used to clean filth from themselves with such relish.

Crumbs fell from Binta's lips as she swallowed and then continued, "All I know is these twisted trees and this dry land—though it is not as dry as those awful cakes—may I have more tea."

Sokhna rolled her eyes, but Alpha simply gestured for Khadi to bring her another cup.

Binta drank the cup in a single gulp before continuing. "As I see it, the question is how long have *you* been here, I was here some days ago and there was no settlement here…"

Sokhna interrupted impatiently, "Make sense you filthy old woman! This village has been here for nine years! How long have you been hiding out there? We've never seen cooking fires coming from beyond those woods!"

"I don't have any use for fires," Binta snarled. Then she licked her lips as a wry smile flashed across her face, "I prefer my meat fresh."

Sokhna gagged, and looked at the woman in sheer horror.

Alpha had heard enough. He motioned for Cherno and his two sons to take Binta by the arm. "We have given due hospitality, and we will not disturb those woods anymore. These young men will walk you to the edge of the village, you can find your way home from there."

Binta snorted in disappointment. "Oh, I see. Fine. I will go. But I have one question for you."

"And what is that?" Alpha asked looking up toward Zamar's bird nest and noticing for the first time that she was gone.

"How did you tame the thing that lives here?" Binta asked, raising a grey eyebrow. "I was here some days ago and it would not let me drink."

"That must have been some time ago," Alpha replied, chuckling. "We draw water freely from the river."

Binta looked puzzled as the boys led her away from the village center. Her head dragged low as if she was sulking, or perhaps confused. She looked as though she was trying to figure out where she was after a very long time sleeping. Suddenly she turned to her left as if she had heard a noise. Then she spun around more quickly than her old body should have allowed and looked directly at Sokhna. "My needy little sister," she shouted, making a pun of Sokhna's name, which sounded like the Wolof word for needs. "Some dreams are real! Maybe the lion really did eat your husband!"

☪

Zamar had flown away as soon as the woman arrived in Alpha's presence. She did not want the jinn that was living behind Binta's eyes to recognize her. Her thoughts raced. How had she missed the presence of one of her kind so close by? Still a hoopoe bird, she flew in the direction that the woman had come from. She came across an empty clay hut that she had seen there before. It was several miles away from the center of the village and in thick woods. But the hut looked as though it had not been inhabited in years. It had almost no roof left at all.

Then Zamar looked more closely and she could see small footpaths around the hut. They led a bit deeper into the woods. It was there that Zamar found Binta's home. It was not a hut at all, whatever was wearing her had made her abandon her hut, and live inside a giant abandoned termite mound lodged into an outcropping of earth deep in the woods. She dissolved from the form of a bird and entered the mound as a still breeze. In the cool darkness of the termite mound, she settled into her natural form and looked around. A badly worn reed mat and an earthen jug of palm wine were the only signs that a human being lived here. The stench was awful. The floor of the cavern was filled with the bones of cane rats, squirrels, and even a wild boar. There was feces everywhere. Zamar fell out of her natural form and became a wind rushing as quickly as she could from the hole in the termite mound. As she came back into daylight, she became an eagle and flew as high as she could to avoid detection.

That night, behind the waterfall, she told Alpha what she had seen. In the hour just before first light, Alpha walked a circle around the village saying prayers of protection and spitting them upon the ground. With Zamar's help, he covered the now wide perimeter of the village more quickly than a swift horse could have, tracing its frontiers with a holy barrier against Binta the Witch.

☪

Sokhna slept uneasily that night. It was Zamar's turn to spend the night with Alpha. Her own children were now old enough to sleep in their own huts, so she was alone. The dream that she used to have before they came to this place, before everything changed, kept coming to her. She saw Alpha squatting beside the river. It was a different Alpha. He did not have the now-familiar handfuls of silver hair on his head or chin. This was the Alpha of days gone by. When he drank from the river the lion attacked as before, but now the lion was jet black with a bright copper mane, and it swallowed Alpha whole! Then the bend of the river itself began to move. The surface of the water became a deep purple snake. It began to curl up and raise its head like a giant cobra, it looked Sokhna right in the eyes and hissed, its tongue flashing out from its toothless mouth. Three times tonight, Sokhna had been awakened just at this point in the dream.

She kept thinking of what Binta had said. *Anyone could have known about the lion, but how did she know about the dream?* Sokhna kept replaying it in her mind. Then she remembered the old woman's joke. She had called out to her calling her Sokhla instead of Sokhna. *But how did she even know my name? No one had said it!*

The next day, after the midday meal, during the hottest part of the day, when the people do not go outside for fear of disturbing spirits, Sokhna snuck out of the village and headed in the direction of Binta's woods.

*

Like Sokhna, Binta was feeling a bit strange on this particular day. She had awakened on her ragged mat on the floor of the termite mound as she had every morning for three decades. Today, no voice inside her had pulled her from sleep. There was no faint buzzing sound, like a swarm of bees flying a few feet away. No. Her mind was strangely silent. She heard the birds singing, and she thirsted for water, not palm wine. She also noticed the smell of the mound, and she was aware that her skin felt itchy. Binta felt the urge to rise from her cavern and go out into the daylight; she thought of going to the river for a drink of cool water, and even a bath.

Ten thousand days had come and gone since she had first come to Futa. And this morning they all seemed to come rushing past her—as if they were one long day or one long dream. To her it seemed that most of the time she had been lost in deep thought or deep conversation. She had figured out the mysteries of the universe, carrying out long, powerful debates in her mind about the nature of men and beasts. She was sure that she had solved each of the riddles of the universe as she sat on the floor of the mound day-by-day and night-by-night. Now, curiously, she could not remember what any of the answers were.

She did manage to recall something of who—or what—she had been before she came to this place. But, no matter how she struggled, she could only form the faintest flicker of an image in her mind's eye. Whenever her thoughts tried to wrap themselves around this memory, it seeped away, like water flowing through her weak, arthritic fingers. All that she could really remember was that she had been running—for her life—she no longer knew who or what she had been trying to escape.

They were chasing me…they wanted to kill me…they said that I had hurt people. They said that I had…eaten people in my sleep. She remembered arriving at the river and being scared away from the banks by a lion, sending her running again. She ran until her legs wouldn't carry her any further and collapsed on the ground waiting to be devoured. When she mustered the courage to look back, she realized that the lion had stopped pursuing her. It was gone; and she was alone. She was lying there next to this enormous termite mound heaving and sweating when she heard what sounded like bees approaching; she was too tired to run anymore.

That was the last time that Binta felt like she did this morning. For the first time in ages Binta Kan was alone.

Binta came out into the daylight, rubbing her eyes to soften the glare. She headed toward the river, and as she passed before the small hut that had once been her home, she realized that her solitude would not last long. There was a woman standing in front of the hut calling out to her in Wolof.

☪

"Old Woman!" Sokhna shouted. "I mean…Grandmother…I mean, Binta. Yes. Grandmother Binta!"

"Are you lost child?" the old woman answered, as she came closer to the door of the hut.

"No." Sokhna said. "I know my way; I came here to see you."

"Ahhh," Binta sighed curiously, "come inside then, I get very few visitors."

Binta wiped ages of dust from two wooden stools and motioned for Sokhna to sit down.

"Something you said to me," Sokhna began, "I want to know what it means…you said that the lion ate my husband…and I…had a dream last night. I don't understand it, but I think you must. I am sure it is about my co-wife. I think she is the lion. I mean, she must have put a spell on him. I mean, I think…"

Binta had been staring at her with confused eyes; finally she interrupted. "My daughter," she said in a raspy, but somehow sweet, hissing voice, "do I know you?"

Now it was Sokhna's turn to stare in confusion. After a moment, she sighed, stood up, and headed to the door. As she reached the threshold, she turned and spoke. Tears were welling in her eyes: "I can see that I have wasted my time, you are obviously soft-headed, or cruel, or both. I don't know, and I don't care. I thought you could help me, my co-wife has bewitched my husband and he has forgotten me."

Now, tears began to flow down Sokhna's cheeks and the words poured from her as well. "For years now, he has forgotten me. I have only ever loved my father and that man, and he doesn't even smile at me anymore. He provides for me and my children, and he…well, he fulfills his duties, but his heart is hers. Since we've come here she brings him twins time and again and my womb gives nothing. I have nothing that he wants anymore. I was the most beautiful girl in Futa. They all came asking for my hand. I only ever wanted him. If I cannot have him back, I don't want to live another day. After what you said, I thought you knew of such things. I thought you could help."

"Please wait," Binta hummed softly, "my sister who has needs. Don't cry. I am sorry I do not remember. I am not myself today. But I…" Binta stammered as she tried to gather her thoughts. "I used to know things. In another life I knew how to do things. I may be able to help you."

Binta looked about the hut furtively, trying to remember a thing long forgotten. Suddenly she stood and hurried to the door and began digging at the earth with the end of her walking stick. Moments later she was wiping the earth away from a handful of cowry shells.

"Tell me," she said, motioning for Sokhna to sit back down, "what is her name?"

"Zamar," Sokhna replied.

"Where does she come from?"

"I do not know," Sokhna answered.

"If you had to guess from looking at her, what land would you say she comes from?" Binta asked.

"She does not look like she came from the land at all," Sokhna said, rolling her eyes, "she looks like something that fell from the sky. She doesn't look like a thing the earth would make."

Binta threw the cowries upon the ground and stared at them. "Your answers puzzle me Sister Sokhla," Binta said, "but it's not so important, as long as you have something from him, something from her, and something for me!"

Sokhna laughed, wiping the tears away from her eyes. "Finally, I've gotten something right! I brought a lock of his hair and the cuttings from his fingernails. And I brought these," Sokhna said, reaching inside of her headwrap to pull out the silver earrings she had carefully tucked away. "He gave them to me as a gift, but I know they were hers so I've never worn them. He brought them back with him from the time that he came here in secret to marry her."

"It's alright child, we'll win him back from her!" Binta exclaimed, "but what have you brought for me."

"I didn't know to bring something for you Grandmother," Sokhna said, unfastening her own gold earrings and bracelet, "but consider these an installment. If you can give him back to me, then all the gold I own is yours!"

Chapter Eleven

THE SANDWRITER

Suddenly Adam and Hawa noticed that the shimmering snake was still there. It was staring at them with new eyes. Gone were the mystery, passion, and longing in its gaze.

It now beheld the man and wife only with cold contempt. Instinctively, the couple shuddered, their flesh crawling ever so slightly. At this, the snake's icy glare broke. Its eyes narrowed, and the corners of its lipless mouth slowly lifted into a sneer.

Wild joy then raced across its face, and it glanced about furtively in anticipation. It was sure it knew what would happen next. Those narrow eyes widened as the Voice bellowed.

The Voice repeated the question they had asked themselves: "What have you done?" He interrogated them about their defiance, and their grave error.

Iblis saw his own scene of rebelliousness flash across his mind's eye. Again he was sure that he knew what would happen next. This time he was wrong.

September 7, 2010 Touba, Senegal

Zamar had left Nemacus screeching in pain inside the Iron dome. When she had snapped off his ear, Jaag called to her to end the interrogation and leave the prisoner. She flew away, her flame roaring, and regained her perch atop the prison. She became an eagle, and sat to gaze across the savanna, as if she were looking into the past. Jaag had made himself clear, Nemacus was to stand trial for his crimes, but Zamar could not simply torture him to settle her own accounts. If she wanted answers, she would need to find them elsewhere. And she knew where to go.

Zamar took wing, and soon she was soaring high above the world of men. At ten thousand feet, the eagle fell away and Zamar became a gust of hot wind, raging east across the face of the world. She flew for hours and hours, punching holes through the clouds as she went. Few of her kind were capable of this. Zamar's special gifts did not begin and end with her ability to pass through iron.

She raced with such speed that the sun refused to set on her. She reached her destination and fell to earth as the sun finally dared to disappear from sight. She lay there, for a while, hidden from the eyes of men, but lying on her side resting from the great voyage. After she had recovered enough strength, she arose and smacked the sandy surface of this strange land with such force that a cloud of dust briefly made her form visible, though there were no humans around to see it. After bathing herself in the fine powder, Zamar, slowly lifted herself above the sand, and began to make the prayer of the traveler, suspended at the pinnacle of the Great Pyramid, as the deep purple sunset reflected off the city of Cairo in the distance.

As she finished her prayer, she felt a familiar gaze upon her. "Peace be upon you Zamar daughter of Nazreel," a rolling voice called out to her in Arabic.

"And upon you peace, Tafaasa, son of the sand, brother of knowledge, companion of timelessness," Zamar replied. It had been a long time since she had spoken the language this way, the old way, instead of speaking the common tongue of the jinn of the south and west.

"It has been a very long time, my child," Tafaasa intoned, "come in from the darkening night of the world of men, and accompany me into the palaces they once raised for us," Tafaasa said, gesturing toward the pyramids. His long lean figure towered over Zamar like a willow-tree made of golden shadows. Tufts of spiky golden hair sprouted from the back of his neck like the tail feathers of a peacock.

"Your invitation is a kind one, dear elder, but I will need your vision tonight. Can we remain out here in the open, where you might see things more clearly?"

"As you wish, Zamar," Tafaasa replied, fixing his hooded, down-turned eyes on her. "But tell me have things changed so much that you traveled thousands of miles to see me? I have seen that Samra'zin the Just and his governors rule the edge of the land now, the place where the sun sets. Do you not find their rule just?"

"The new lords of the western jinn are not just! They are only jinn."

"But things have changed for the good, have they not?"

"Just because one is not manifestly committed to evil does not make one good."

"True. But, when given the choice between bad and worse, one must favor the bad," Tafaasa reasoned.

"When the great teachers of the humans came, they drew lines around their cities of Radiance and Repentance nonetheless to keep out Samra'zin and his jinn."

"This is true our daughter, but they do let some of us through, do they not?" He said raising a golden eyebrow.

"Yes. But it has always been so. Even when Nazreel sought their demise, some of our kind were welcomed among their people of knowledge."

"Why then, do you resist the new Sultan and his ways and laws?"

"Elder, I do not long for the days of my father, but is it really a crime to hide who I was…who I have been? Their laws made me an fugitive, just for having once loved a man. To live in peace in their land, I had to hide. I betrayed my lost love every day…the marriage that we made, the feelings that I had for him. The home that we made together, the love that we shared…the children," sobs robbed Zamar of her voice.

"You ask questions that have no answers, my child," Tafaasa began somberly, "only one judge can hear such cases, and His Hearing has not yet come."

"Will it come at all?" Zamar sighed.

"You lose faith?"

"I do not know anymore. Perhaps my deeds were major sins, and I have spent these past centuries paying for them. I do not know. But He made me to love him! I pray that this is penance, for I cannot live with the idea that I have suffered so greatly for nothing. Please tell me that He is there, and that His justice is true. These were truths that I once knew, but time and pain has covered them over."

"Every morsel of flesh, and every flicker of flame has its purpose Zamar. You cannot forget this," said Tafaasa gently. "His plan was for us to be incomplete and weak servants, He knows best why. To question it is in our nature, but to resent it is rebellion."

"May God preserve us from rebellion, and from the fate of our forefather who rebelled," Zamar exclaimed. "I have not abandoned the road, but I walk it with little strength, and even less faith."

"When you first crashed to the earth here all those years ago, you were almost dead. You were fleeing for your life, covered with shattered jinn and beasts, and you bathed in agony of the soul. You sought redemption and guidance, but then, as now, I can provide only one of these."

"Then give me guidance my teacher, for I am lost," Zamar cried, "the past has returned to haunt me, and though this is what I prayed for ardently, now that it has come, it mocks and curses me."

"You speak of Nemacus," Tafaasa said, quietly.

Zamar's eyes widened. "You know something of this?" she asked.

Tafaasa nodded his great slim head, the wispy whiskers above his eyes dipped slightly as his brow furrowed: "I saw the signs of his return. His footfalls had not been felt on this side of the ocean in a very long time. The sands carried their vibrations."

"And what did the sands tell you?" Zamar asked.

"Very little, Zamar," Tafaasa said slowly, "but I knew that he was alive, and that he had returned to the lands at the edge of the world."

"You saw what happened?"

"No my child," Tafaasa replied kindly, "but seeing you again here after all these many years…well, let us say that I did not need the gift of sight to know that he must be the cause of your torments."

Zamar nodded.

"Do you wish to tell me of what has happened?" Tafaasa asked.

"Dear Elder, I cannot speak of the painful past," Zamar sighed, "I flew all this way to find the road forward. Please help me!"

☾

Tafaasa raised his right arm high above his head and invoked God's name, calling upon Him as the Knowing. *"Bismillahi al-'Alim."* Then, he lowered that hand rapidly and in a single gesture swept it across the surface of the sand without touching it. The crystals of sand began to move about like iron filings being dragged by a magnet. His eyes were closed. He swept his right hand time and again, sometimes quickly, sometime slowly. When he passed his hand slowly, his seven fingers fluttered over the earth, causing the sand to dance.

Zamar's eyes widened as Tafaasa the Sandwriter brushed his right arm over the canvas of the desert floor. First, she saw almond shaped-eyes appear and then vanish again. Then, thick eyebrows and a smooth forehead appeared in the sands only to disappear. Now, a full nose was taking shape in the middle of a slim oval shaped face. This was a human face. Suddenly the eyes returned, the nose, the brow, and the lips. The face was unmistakably familiar. The sands were still. Zamar's mind raced and her heart sobbed as she looked upon the face of her long lost love, Alpha.

☾

"W…What…Why did you draw him?" Zamar asked, stammering.

"Shh…be still child," Tafaasa whispered, with only a hint of impatience.

Tafaasa's brow was furrowed, straining to clear his mind and allow the image to flow directly to his hand. With his eyes still closed, Tafaasa swept clear a palate of sand just to the left of the face that was sculpted on the desert floor.

His fingers dangled downward like the tips of a reed pen awaiting inspiration. Tafaasa was motionless, and for a moment Zamar looked up from the face of her beloved, to see if something was wrong. Tafaasa was completely still, almost like the frozen statues she interrogated in the Iron Dome. Tafaasa was being held prisoner, awaiting an image that would free him. Suddenly his hand burst into motion, sweeping rapidly across the sand and leaving behind four unconnected Arabic letters: *sha—raa—yaa—faa*.

Sharif.

Zamar knew the word—eminent, noble, well-bred—but she did not understand what it meant. This was a title that was usually used for those among men who claimed descent from the Holy Prophet. *What does it have to do with Alpha? I never heard of him making such a claim.*

"I am finished. You may ask your questions." Tafaasa said, seemingly spent from the task.

"Why have you drawn my dead husband?" Zamar asked.

"My gifted young daughter," Tafaasa exclaimed, "there is much that you do not understand. I cannot draw the dead. The sand only writes of those that swim, walk, or fly in the worlds of the living."

"I do not understand. Do not speak in riddles!" Zamar said loudly, then she hushed her voice so that it did not travel with the desert wind. "Speak to me plainly dear Elder, are you saying that my Alpha is alive? I saw his body! Do not torment me! He died ages ago."

"Zamar," Tafaasa intoned, "I love you too much to torment you. There is much I do not know about the images that write themselves on the sand through me. But I know three things: that this cannot be your husband. The sand tells me that this man, Sharif, is the fruit of your womb. He still draws breath today, somewhere very far away from here.

☪

Before she quite knew what was happening, Zamar was in full flight again. She had thanked Tafaasa and sped away. If what he said was true, then she would get her answers from Nemacus whether or not Jaag permitted it. She would dismember him piece by frozen piece, or she would return him to his jinn form and cut him to ribbons with iron until his flame gave out. Even Jaag would not stop her. She resolved that if she had to, she would kill her husband the warden, all the soldiers, all the governors and Samra'zin himself. Her father had long tried to convince her to use the deadly potential of her extraordinary gifts, but Zamar detested violence; she had lived her whole life trying not to harm any of God's creatures. But once long ago, she had learned how deadly she could be. As she climbed the skies she made a terrible promise. *Before the next sunset, I will bring the Angel of Death to the jinn of the west—if I must—to have my answers. Nemacus will tell me if some of my seed really are alive!*

It was still the dead of night. This time she flew directly up through the clouds, to the top of the skies, passing in front of a passenger jet and racking it with turbulence. At 35,000 feet, she continued to climb higher and higher until there was no more sky left. Zamar had never flown so high before; she had never even thought to fly so high before. She had only heard of a few jinn even able to climb so high into the heavens. *This will be an easier way home, and for the fight that awaits me, I will need to conserve my energy.*

Before long, Zamar had left the turning of the world behind. She was alone and quiet in the blackness of space with only scattered thoughts, memories, and stars to keep her company. *How can it be true? None of them survived. How could they have survived? I saw their bodies!* There she hung outside the earth's orbit, suspended in her ethereal form, watching all the tragedies of her long life pass before her mind's eye. And, so she waited for the hours to pass, for her homeland—her answers—to be brought back round to her by the timeless turning of the earth.

☪

September 8, 2010 Touba, Senegal

The time had come. She opened her eyes, and looked down at the vast blue, white, and brown sphere below her. For a moment, Zamar searched the earth in vain, and wondered if she would be able to find her way home from so high above everything she knew. But, after a moment, she spotted her target. It looked like a giant earthen spiral in the otherwise featureless Sahara. She saw it whenever she flew high above the desert near her home. She had read about it in her father's ledgers a very long time ago. And Zamar never forgot *anything* that she read, so she was now one of very few to know what this place had once been.

The jinn that first came here to the lands of the West, many, many thousands of eons ago had given it a name in the ancient tongue. When the Arabs first came, some learned what this name meant from the jinn that visited, and they called this spot, the *Qalb al-irshaad*, "center of guidance." The children of Adam now called it the *Guelb er-Richat*, and said that it meant "the heart of the desert bird." Still, its original name told of its original purpose. It had been worn into a swirling target on the desert floor in an age when there were many more jinn that roamed the skies, and this mark on the land guided them. They used it to find the place where the jinn of the Western lands dwelled. It was the place that they fell back to earth, and the place where they whirled themselves into a wind to propel back into the skies. Over eons of use, it had taken the appearance of a giant bulls-eye from the air and Zamar would now revive its ancient purpose. She became a wind—a white-hot downdraft from the heavens—and she plunged toward the center of guidance with frightening speed.

☾

An old shepherd, grazing his herd in the early hours of the morning in the light grasses that grew at the edges of the Geulb was nearly knocked off of his feet. His animals bleated wildly as they were momentarily blinded by sand in their eyes. A couple of Swedish backpackers were camped in the valley, and their tent was toppled over entirely by this hot desert wind that seemed to arise out of nowhere. Blazing sand and dust blew in every direction.

Zamar had landed.

The sun had not yet come over the horizon, and washing her airy form in the dust, she made her morning prayer at the very core of the heart of right guidance. She prayed to God that His Will be done, and asked His protection against her enemies from among the jinn and the men. Knowing that this might be the last sunrise she would witness, she took extra time to beg for forgiveness for her sins. At peace with her self, her sins, and her soul, Zamar rushed over the surface of the earth. She sped toward the iron-domed prison hidden in the earthen ruins a few miles outside of Touba, the city of Repentance.

☪

As Zamar approached the iron-dome, she knew something was terribly wrong. Nothing was moving, neither jinn nor man, and a fine white powder covered the spot where the old walls of the prison should have stood. It was as if some dreadful tornado had just struck hours before, and the dust had only now finished settling. The prison had been leveled.

Zamar flew through the small hole and narrow earthen corridor that led to the iron-dome. Nemacus was gone.

Just then, she heard a whimper coming from her left in a far dark corner of the iron cage.

"Peace…p…peace to you…Zamar," the voice called, barely audible.

She spun about to see one of the most truly awful things that she had ever seen—and hers had already been a long and tragic life. She could make out a head, hardened like a rock, in the half-light of the cage, but as she took in the rest of the figure that was frozen solid and slumped on its belly in the corner, she realized that much of it was missing. This jinn had been cut almost in half. Most of its left side was crumbled dust and one of its eyes had been removed. Its right leg was completely detached and lay shattered across its back, as though his tormentors had beaten him with his own severed limb. It was her husband, Jaag.

"Peace be upon you my poor husband," Zamar cried, choking on the words.

"God answers prayers, and I have hope for my soul," Jaag said in a crackling, agonized whisper. "In the hours since they left, I only asked Him to forgive me for all the things I have done at this place, and to let me set eyes on you one more time."

Zamar began to sob, remembering that only hours ago she had sworn to kill him if she had to. Seeing him like this, she could only remember all his kindness to her. He always had endless patience for her moods, her whims, and even her secrets. Jaag had always loved her far more than she had ever been able to love him. Seeing him like this, petrified in the pain of what was surely one of the most ghastly deaths ever suffered by a jinn, she realized that she had cheated him.

"Shh…my husband," she finally said, "try not to speak. I will get you out of here."

"Zamar," Jaag began, "this iron cage is the only thing keeping me alive. The things they have done to me are things that no jinn can survive. These few words are all I have left. Please accept them."

"As you wish my love," Zamar replied.

"They…they came for him," Jaag began, "the Elementals. We thought we were ready. Never have I seen so many, and never have I seen such ruthlessness. Sangoot is dead. All the guards are dead. Everyone is dead."

"Bounty hunters! They came to claim the reward for him?" Zamar asked.

"No my love," Jaag moaned, "they did not even take the treasure that is hidden here, I begged them to take it in exchange for Sangoot's life. They cared nothing for fortune."

"What kind of bounty hunters do not care for jewels and riches?"

"My beautiful wife, these were no bounty hunters. They came for Nemacus. He commanded them. He commanded that they…do *this* to me. They were his soldiers, his army. They were his…children."

The mourning flicker in Zamar's breast became a raging flame as she took in the meaning of Jaag's dying words. Nemacus had been breeding these elementals to raise an army! He had been teaching and training them for a war not only against men, but against jinn.

"I am sorry my husband," Zamar said. "Please forgive me. I was never the wife I should have been for you. I was keeping secrets from you."

"Don't be ridiculous Zamar," Jaag said, managing a laugh, "I knew of your human husband all along. Al-Hajj, the father of your bounty hunter friend, Ben Al-Hajj told me long ago. I did not want you to tell me until you were ready. I kept your secret from Samra'zin and his kind. I never betrayed you, just as I knew you would never betray me. You were faithful to me; it is no sin for your heart to stay faithful to your first love as well."

"I love you Jaag," Zamar whispered.

"And I love you Zamar," Jaag responded. "And since you love me I must ask you two final terrible favors."

"Anything my love," Zamar said, stroking his hand.

"You must take my fire now. They wanted to leave me in a living hell like this, please put me out of my misery. And when you have finished me, unchain your gifts and avenge me. Only you can stop the monstrosity that Nemacus is preparing to unleash on the world."

Chapter Twelve

SACRIFICE

Noble, honest, and filled with the deepest regret, Adam and Hawa spoke the truth. With one voice they said, "Oh our Lord! Surely we have wronged ourselves! If You do not forgive us, and show us mercy, surely we will be among the losers."

Their Lord forgave them.

Now forgiven, still the Lord cast them out. They were meant to know the Garden, but not to reside in it until after the horn had blown. The Earth was to be theirs, to live for a time, and to toil for a livelihood.

Robbed of his vengeance, Iblis began to see that he had underestimated the man and wife. Still blinded by hate, he too was cast upon the Earth, where he swore to continue his war.

February 20, 1774 CE,
Saint Louis Island
Eighth day of Dhul-Hijjah, 1187 AH

Governor Thomas O'Meara swung the wooden doors of his spacious bungalow wide open to let in the cool night air. He was bathed in sweat, and here on the veranda of the second story bedroom, there was always an ocean breeze. The sweet smoky scent of hardwood fires wafted in the wind. He wrapped his robe around himself and stepped outside to light his pipe, cupping his hands to keep the flame from flickering. He was still panting a bit, and his breath extinguished the first match, "son of a bitch!" he said, before succeeding in lighting the pipe on his second attempt. The kept woman lying across the bed pulled the sheets up over herself to cover her nakedness, and shouted something at him in the language of the country, "*Tejjal ma bunt ba, nelawu guddi ga seddna guy.*"

"Speak English God damn it! You know quite well that I do not speak nigger." O'Meara said, turning to curse her a bit slower than he had intended. The semen and sweat on his bulbous stomach had congealed, cementing his robe to his body and making it even harder than usual to move his corpulent frame.

The woman on the bed called out to him again in all the English she could muster—which was mixed with very broken French: "Close ze porte, it makes cold zis night."

"Oh, very well," O'Meara said with a scoff, slamming the doors behind him as he stepped outside to smoke his pipe in peace. He looked out over Saint Louis Island. From this balcony he could look to his right and see the ocean, just past the fine candlelit homes of the French and mulatto slave-traders. The last bit of the sunset was disappearing from the sky and the waxing moon had risen. In its light he could see the white waves cresting on a boundless black sea.

Somewhere beyond those waves was the American mainland with its mounds of tobacco, and the American islands with their endless fields of sugar cane. A world of riches was out there somewhere across that vast expanse of blackness. And it all depended on the vast expanse of blackness that teemed in the lands to his left. Turning to face away from the sea, he could just make out the cooking fires of the natives on the mainland. He took it all in, and drew sharply from his pipe. Then he exhaled with deep satisfaction, believing himself the master of all he surveyed.

His Wolof courtesan had gratified him tonight. *She's a bit too old and black to please the eyes,* he thought, chuckling to himself. *But she knows just how to please the other parts!* He inhaled again quickly, but exhaled slowly, watching the smoke as the night air carried it away. *If things go well on the expedition to Futa, in two days time I'll have some new light-skinned nigger girls to play with. I bet there will be a virgin or two in the bunch...*

The bleating of sheep broke into his fantasy. For the natives, the day after tomorrow would be the greatest feast of the year, the festival of the sacrifice. Lambs, sheep, rams, and goats had been pouring into the island's native quarters for a month now in anticipation. O'Meara muttered aloud to no one in particular: "Honestly, you can smell their dung and hear their infernal bleating even in the civilized parts of this God-forsaken island! I should make a law about those bloody lambs and their pagan ceremony!"

He tried to resume his imaginary conquests of heathen virgins, but the moment was gone. All he could think about was tomorrow's expedition and all the noise being made by the sheep. *Lambs to the slaughter...all of them* he chuckled as he finished his pipe. *I had better get that black bitch out of my bed and get a few hours of sleep. We set sail at midnight.*

☪

As the moon made its way across the night sky, O'Meara and his men rowed their canoes out to the large wooden slave ship anchored in the harbor at the mouth of the Senegal River. A dozen at a time, they came aboard, until there were nearly eighty of them aboard the ship. She was an oceangoing sailing vessel that could tack against the wind. She also had a full galley to row for speed against the current or in pursuit of other ships. Most importantly, she was rigged for slaving, with wooden rafters and irons below deck to keep captives chained, and cannons mounted all along her sides. In this, the middle of the dry season, the rifles, shot, and powder could all be stored above deck, since the rains were still months away. The low water level in the river this time of year would pose a bit of a challenge, but with an experienced sailor like O'Meara at the helm, it would easily be able to travel several hundred miles inland in the still and deep waters of the Senegal. She was called the *Jezebel*.

Tonight, *Jezebel* would not have to travel that far. The letter from the black Prince—Ayubba Sulay— said that the swelling village was just past Fort Dagana, one hundred ticks upriver. This prince had sent his emissaries to St. Louis Island a few weeks earlier, and offered this whole village against the debts that he had incurred to O'Meara for last year's imports of guns, rum, silk, and horses. More importantly, the envoys had explained to O'Meara's black interpreters that the negroes in this village were insurrectionists. They were among those who were rising to fight against the Cheddo, the Princes, and the White Men. If villages like this one were allowed to thrive, they argued, soon O'Meara would have no trade in negroes at all.

O'Meara cared nothing for such arguments. All he needed to know was that if he raided the village, there would be no reprisals from the local princes. Once his interpreters explained this to him in broken English, he wanted only for them to point the town out on a map.

And here he was, holding that map in his hand, barking out orders to the *Jezebel's* motley crew. Tonight and all day tomorrow they would sail to Fort Dagana. They would pass the night there and attack the natives at dawn on their holiday. The crew repeated and explained the orders to one another in English, French, Wolof, Bambara, and Portuguese creole. Some were white, some were black, and most were every shade in between. Only a few of the white men were O'Meara's commissioned officers and soldiers. An expedition such as this was—strictly speaking—illegal according to British law. As Governor, O'Meara was forbidden to trade slaves on his own account; he was to administer the colony and trade for the crown. But London was far away, and he knew that the dozen soldiers with him tonight were every bit as dirty as he was and would never report anything.

He always gave each man a share of the spoils, and pretended to be their comrade and partner in crime. On this expedition each officer had been promised at least two slaves. But their greed was not the source of O'Meara's confidence. No. The Governor left nothing to chance: He had something on each and every one of them. If ever they tried to go straight—and lived to tell of it—he could make sure that they spent the rest of their lives rotting in a dungeon.

The rest of the men were—like the British officers themselves—filthy dregs floating in the putrid foam of the Atlantic. They had washed up from everywhere. There were Frenchmen and Dutchmen, Portuguese and Spaniards. Some had been pirates, some dreamed to be. Among the many shades of mulattoes and mestizos were Brazilians and

Jamaicans, Angolans and Cape Verdeans. Many were half-caste bastards that had been born in or around the Islands of St. Louis or Gorée. More than a few were the sons of slave women gang-raped by sailors. They had no fathers, or rather they had too many. Some had no maternal kin either, their natural mothers had died of syphilis or cholera in their youths and they had managed to survive only by being willing to steal or kill when others were not.

Finally there were the negroes: Some were still slaves, others had bought their own freedom with the money from slaves they had kidnapped. Some were criminals sold to the coast after being convicted of murder or rape, sodomy or witchcraft. They came from all up and down the African coast. Each one had once lived a story of loss, suffering, and shame. Now they dealt these to others.

☪

February 21, 1774 CE, Jamtan
Ninth day of Dhul-Hijjah, 1187 AH

Alpha had been fasting all day. It was the Day of Arafat, the last day of the rites of the Pilgrimage to Mecca, and the day before the biggest holiday of the year. All day long Alpha had been walking alongside the pilgrims in his mind. Though they were thousands of miles away, every step he took that day was with them. When he walked up the riverbank to visit his sheep, he was climbing the Mount of Mercy. When he sat beneath the tree to hear the supplications of the people, he sat alongside the pilgrims. And while he abstained from food and drink from the time of the cool dawn through the day's stifling heat, he was praying that one day God would allow him to make his own pilgrimage.

When the sun was just beginning to come down from its highest point in the sky, Alpha began to feel faint, the way he had when he fasted as a boy. He went to the basin in the courtyard to make his ablutions, hoping that the splash of water on his face would refresh him. There on the surface of the water he saw the reflection of the Ka'aba, the house in Mecca that Abraham and Ishmael had made for the worship of God. He was sure he was hallucinating. Alpha rubbed his eyes and looked into the basin again, and still there before him was the cube-shaped House of God. He dipped his hand in the water, and the image vanished. He splashed the cool water on his face, and began purifying himself for the prayer.

The mosque at Jamtan was now a large, two story earthen structure. The young men had been building it since the last rainy season, bringing baskets of fine silt from the bottom of the river to plaster its mud walls. Today it was full. Alpha led at least 200 of the village's men, and at least 100 of its women in the noon prayer. At the end of the prayer, he sat to lead them in supplication. He said prayers of peace upon the Prophet, time and time again.

As he said the prayers, his thoughts drifted across the miles and the centuries back to the Prophet's farewell sermon, the last time he gave a speech to the pilgrims, the very last time he made the pilgrimage before passing away. He spoke to the people briefly about this, reminding them that on that day almost 1200 years ago, the Prophet told the people, "Today God has perfected for you your religion." Then he reminded them that the Prophet's message that day was for everyone in the whole world: "And there is no preference for the Arab over the non-Arab, nor for the non-Arab over the Arab."

As he spoke the words, he scanned the crowd to meet eyes with the dozens of Moorish disciples who had left the desert in the past nine years to come serve him and learn from him. It was then that he noticed a bright-skinned, bearded man sitting alone, leaning on one of the large wooden pillars at the back of the mosque. This man was clearly an Arab, but he did not remember being introduced to him. Most of the men were fasting this day, and many looked haggard, but this man's clothes and face were fresh.

Alpha abruptly ended the supplications and began rushing through the crowd toward the back of the mosque. The people kept stopping him to shake his hand, or for him to spit his prayers into their outstretched hands. But each time he looked up, he locked eyes knowingly with the Arab stranger at the back of the mosque. The man's eyes were kind, and they smiled at Alpha each time that he looked back. Finally, when Alpha had almost made his way through the mass of humanity that crowded the mosque that day, he looked back to the pillar to find the strange Arab with the kind eyes. This time, the man was gone.

☪

Zamar had spent the day in human form, playing with her children in what was now her husband's village. They all played together. The two older sets of twins did not go to the Qur'an school this day. They had been off since the month began to prepare for the holiday. Today they played right alongside their baby sisters at the bank of the river, only a few steps away from the spot where Alpha had subdued Zamar with God's words nine years before.

"I am going to eat so much lamb I won't be able to move!" shouted Tamsir.

"Well, I am going to eat so much lamb that I won't be able to talk!" Echo cooed.

"Each of you will have plenty of meat, your father has made sure of it," Zamar said, smiling. "And there will be figs, and fruits, and dates, and honey!"

But the oldest pair of twins had already run off, racing one another in the sand along the side of the river.

"Mmmm, I love honey Mama," said Hush.

"Me too, Mama, me too!" cried Whisper. Zamar's twin baby girls were now three years old and toddling about, talking, and eating all the time. She could only laugh at their declaration of love for honey.

"I know little ones, I know," she said, "it is almost as sweet as the two of you." Whisper and Hush smiled at one another, and began skipping in circles a few yards away from the river bank.

"Mama said stay away from the water you two!" the twin boys Samba and Demba shouted in unison.

"You're not anyone's daddy!" Whisper and Echo shouted back in their tiny childlike voices.

"Now girls," Zamar began, choking back laughter. "Your brothers are right, you stay away from the banks, you hear?"

"Yes Mama," said the girls, as they went back to whirling around in circles before falling to the ground giggling.

"And you, Samba and Demba," Zamar said, calling out to the boys, who were waiting for their seventh birthday to come in a little over a month, "do you not like honey?"

Samba and Demba looked up from their game of Wuri, and looked at each other before answering with one voice: "we like *honey* just fine Mama, but we're *men* now, we are going to have a man's share of *meat*!"

Zamar laughed so hard that the pointy teeth at the back of her mouth shone in the sun.

"Mama!" the boys cried—again in unison—"we *are* men now, father taught us how to shoot a slingshot."

"Of course, my sons," Zamar said, wiping her eyes and trying to make her face serious. "You are brave hunters. You must eat your share of meat to keep up your strength."

"That's right," said Samba, sternly.

"Soon we will hunt our own gazelles and share the meat with you Mama," Demba continued, elaborating on the point. Then he wrapped his knuckles against the wooden game board to remind his brother that it was his turn to play. Samba nodded, and placed a smooth pebble in one of the holes closest to the top of the board. And with that the boys were off, making move after move with lightning speed, the pebbles making a clacking rhythm as their speedy competition unfolded.

Though the boys were no longer really listening, Zamar called out nonetheless: "Just remember what I told you, do not shoot at birds with those slingshots, you never know what you might hit."

"Yes Mama," the boys shouted absent-mindedly, engrossed as they always were in competition with one another.

Just then Tamsir and Echo had returned from their long race. Echo, the older of the two by seconds, was leading her younger brother the whole way, until Tamsir entered a furious closing sprint, his feet flying like those of a horse, barely touching the sand at all. The eldest pair of twins were neck and neck as they lost their balance and tumbled in the sand at the shady spot where Zamar was sitting on her reed mat.

"I win!" they both cried.

"What!?" Tamsir shouted, "Mama, tell her I won!"

"No! Mama, tell him I won!" Echo replied.

Then the twins looked at one another, covered as they were with sand, and began to laugh riotously.

"Look Mama," Echo shouted, grabbing a handful of sand, and squeezing it tightly, before opening her hand to reveal a shiny glass bead, "I've been practicing!"

"Me too, Mama, look!" Tamsir shouted, opening both hands to reveal two shiny rough glass beads.

"Good children!" Zamar, said laughing with joy. "You are special. Your talents are just beginning to show, I have so much to teach you."

And so they spent the afternoon, with Zamar's wild cackling laughter rippling through the air every few minutes as her beautiful children wrestled and raced, teased and taunted, skipped and sang.

☾

The peals of laughter finally stopped in the late afternoon. Sokhna was happy to hear the silence. She knew that it meant that Zamar was leaving the village to go back to her own compound, wherever that was. Though she was glad that her rival was leaving, she began to complain out loud: "How come that girl never spends a night in this village hmm?" she said, absent-mindedly turning around expecting to see Khadija rolling her eyes.

Then Sokhna realized that this evening, her eldest daughter Khadija was not here to politely scold her for her jealousy of Zamar, nor to remind her that Alpha was a good husband and father. They had married Khadija off nearly two months ago, to the son of one of Alpha's old teachers. The wise old sage from Saalum, not far from the Gambia River, had taught Alpha the arts of poetry long ago. The youngest of his sons, Aliun Cissé was now in his mid twenties and had spent years studying in Jamtan. He had been smitten with Khadija's intelligence and beauty. It was no secret that Khadija was as taken with him as he was with her. When Aliun returned to Saalum almost a year earlier, Khadija had cried on Sokhna's shoulder.

When he came back two months ago bearing gifts of books, cattle, and incense as his dowry, Khadija was giddy. But Alpha imposed a condition before he would allow Aliun—whom he liked very much—to marry his daughter.

"Son of Saalum," Alpha had said, "you will be *my* son if—and only if—you swear never to stand between my daughter and knowledge."

"Father of wisdom," Aliun had responded, "I pray that you will be *my* father as well. I respect whatever conditions you impose, but you should know that I wish to marry your daughter only so that she can teach me from her knowledge! I have no time for a pretty, empty-headed girl!" Alpha had smiled and embraced the young man tightly, but Sokhna was sure that she had seen a tear on Alpha's cheek that day as he saw his eldest daughter climb aboard the donkey for the long ride to Saalum.

☪

As the sun began to set that night, it was Sokhna's turn to miss their daughter. Khadija was not so much younger than Sokhna herself. The two had long been as much close friends as mother and daughter. Even the strain of Sokhna's jealousy of Zamar, and her resentment of Alpha had not been able to break their bond. Khadija defended her father *and* she loved her mother. But with Khadija now gone, there was nothing to temper Sokhna's anger and jealousy. Instead of keeping good company with her wise daughter, she was often going to see the strange old woman Binta instead.

As this evening fell, Binta was all that Sokhna could think about. She let her maids prepare the children for the feast tomorrow and she kept herself locked up in her hut. She sat on her bed, affectionately caressing the small red charm that Binta had made for her while she waited for the sun to set. Alone in her room, she reminded herself of the steps that Binta had outlined to make her spell against Zamar take its effect. *We will see if she is still his favorite when her womb is barren*, she thought.

When the sun finally went down, and the others in the compound headed to the mosque to pray the sunset prayer, Sokhna came out of her hut, grabbed the old red rooster from the courtyard and brought it back to her room. She pulled the wooden shutters closed, hung the dark crimson charm around her neck, and pulled a sharp knife from underneath her bed. She had slit a rooster's throat before, but never without pronouncing God's name, and never with an intention other than to feed her family or her guests. This was different. Sokhna began to say the strange words that Binta had taught her, and she pulled the knife firmly across the bird's neck. Soon the blood was trickling down, falling in streams and drops on a mound of locks of copper-colored hair, stolen from each of Zamar's six children.

☪

February 21, 1774 CE, Fort Dagana
Ninth day of Dhul-Hijjah, 1187 AH

It was just before midnight on a dark and cloudy night. Neither moon nor star shone in the sky. On O'Meara's orders the crew of the *Jezebel* slept on the deck of the ship rather than in Dagana's small fort, just in case of a surprise attack from the natives. Aside from those who kept the watch, almost all obeyed the Governor's command to bed down early. There was little for them to do anyway. Fort Dagana had no whores, and as a precaution O'Meara had secretly removed all the rum from the ship to ensure a disciplined and well-rested crew.

So tonight, his two-legged beasts slept well. But these experienced murderers and manhunters did not sleep alone on the deck of the *Jezebel*. Nor were they even the most dangerous things present that night on the boat. Unseen, even by those who kept the watch, were other creatures that likewise plotted harm against God's creations. Nemacus, Sultan Nazreel, and an unseen army of jinn had come aboard at Dagana. They floated alongside them, hovered above them, and swam in and out of them. And the cargo hold of the *Jezebel* this night was filled with an invisible company of jinn, elementals, and half-breed beasts.

There too was Luemba, the thing that had worn Binta the Witch for nearly thirty years. When O'Meara gave his final reminder to the crew on how the dawn attack on was to unfold, Luemba explained to Nazreel the way to find his long lost daughter. And Nazreel and Nemacus dispensed the orders on how to overcome the village's defenses, and slay its jinn protector, Zamar the Betrayer.

☪

February 22, 1774 CE, Jamtan
10ᵗʰ Day of Dhul-Hijjah, 1187 AH

Assan the Hunchbacked Muezzin awakened in a cold sweat. He had been having a terrible nightmare and even awake the hairs on the back of his neck still stood on end. He did not think anything of it. He often felt like something was pulling him from sleep just before the first crow of the cock, and just before the first light showed like a white thread strung across the black horizon. Assan prided himself not only on his beautiful *adhan* but on the fact that he almost never called it late. Something inside him made the *adhan* in his heart every morning just before the break of dawn, and this usually made him smile. This morning, he was not smiling. He rubbed his eyes and emerged from his hut to look east at the horizon. There was still nothing there, but he knew it was close. Jamtan was perfectly still. All of the women had been up late sewing clothes for the Tabaski, and the men had been up late drinking tea and talking to one another about all the miraculous events of the past year, indeed the past nine years. Everyone slept, putting their morning prayer safely in Assan's capable hands. As always, he would awaken them when it was time to give glory to God.

Assan took his washbasin and began to make his ablutions, but as he closed his eyes to wash his face, he saw the terrifying lizard-like eyes that he had seen in his nightmare. *La ilaha illa Allah.* Assan said in his mind. *I must be getting weak-minded in my old age; here I am being spooked by a bad dream like a little boy spending his first night away from mama at the Qur'an school!* As he rinsed his feet and placed them back in his sandals, Assan looked again to the east and saw the faintest light peeking over the horizon.

Sunrise was still well over an hour away, but the time to call the people to pray had arrived.

Assan climbed the short wooden ladder to the tower of the little clay mosque in the center of Jamtan. He began clearing his throat as he reached the top rung, but suddenly he started to cough uncontrollably. Dust was in the back of his throat. Dust was whirling everywhere. A furious wind had begun to whip through the town, and Assan rubbed his eyes to try to see what was going on. Suddenly Assan felt like he was being surrounded by a hot, dusty whirlwind. The ladder began to waver beneath him, and before he knew it, Assan the hunchback was being hurled toward the ground with unspeakable force. The last thing he heard was a cracking sound as his skull smashed against the heavy stone just outside the mosque, the one that people rubbed in place of ablutions when they arrived very late for the prayer.

The whirlwind that had enveloped him slowed, then stopped, and finally poured itself into the form of Nemacus. His cold lizard-like eyes surveyed the village in the darkness. Then the other violent breezes that were rushing through the town began to whip around him before settling into their natural shapes. Nemacus stared out at the airy forms of no fewer than one hundred jinn.

"You know your orders," he hissed. "Make a ruin of this place. The flesh dealers will arrive here soon. You are to help them destroy this place in any way that you can. Wear them if you need to. Guide them if they will let you. If you are able to help them kill, do so. The one we are here for will be one of the mature men. Kill any of these that you can, but if you see one with a scar along his right temple, do whatever you can to murder it. That fleshling must die here tonight or Sultan Nazreel will extinguish each and every one of you!"

The small battalion of jinn nodded in silent assent. Nemacus continued, "When Sultan Nazreel and the main legions are finished with Zamar, the traitor, they will come with the beasts and the half-breeds and join us here. The Old Witch and her apprentice have broken their *holy seal*," said Nemacus, spitting fire at the ground in contempt. "The apprentice made a blood sacrifice here last night in my name. They can no longer keep us out. Today, we will have our victory! Today we annihilate the one that was foretold! Tonight we exterminate the filthy ball of mud that wants to destroy us!"

C·

Less than two hundred yards up the river, another general rallied his troops. "Don't kill more of the men than you must," O'Meara shouted. "They're not worth anything dead. And ravage the married women if you want, but the virgins are mine! Understood? If any of you dare to take what's mine I will cut off his member myself!"

The light of dawn was just now beginning to make the world visible. "This is the spot," O'Meara shouted. "Ready the anchor! Landing party, prepare the canoes. Cannons at the ready! When we pass the bend of the river, the village will be in sight. Be prepared to fire!"

The *Jezebel* slowly rolled around the bend of the river, and as night gave way to day the men could see the minaret on the little clay mosque in the middle of Jamtan, not far from the banks of the river. There were a hundred little clay huts dotting the south bank. Except for a sandstorm that left rippling eddies of dust whirling through the lanes of the town, nothing seemed to move.

"Drop anchor!" O'Meara cried. The ship, which had been moving slowly anyway came to a stop and reversed its course with the gentle flow of the river. "Ready!" O'Meara shouted once the ship had settled. "Aim!" he continued. The men were already bristling with excitement, and now their hearts began to race. The men at the cannons directed them toward the mosque and the largest dwellings in the little earthen town. "Fire!"

☾

Alpha awoke with a strange feeling. He could see the faintest traces of light in the sky, but he had not heard Assan's voice. Something was wrong. He could feel it. Alpha Ba did something he had not done in years. He reached under his bed and pulled out his machete. He then reached for the silver dagger with the Qur'an verses inscribed along the handle that Zamar had found in the vault in the desert nine years before. He pulled on a short tan barkcloth tunic and slipped out of his hut to see what was going on. He looked toward the mosque and saw dust settling next to what looked like the figure of a man slumped outside the front door. Then he looked to the river and saw masts on a large ship. Finally, the sound of horrible explosions ripped open the peace of the dawn.

Cannonballs fell on Jamtan like rain. The minaret crumbled, the roofs and walls of huts collapsed. Women screamed. Children cried. Then came the fire. Three catapult shots of Greek Fire hit the town and exploded, setting two dozen homes alight. The people came running from their homes, some engulfed in flames.

Alpha immediately ran toward the river. Cherno was emerging from his hut with three rifles in hand. He passed one to Alpha, along with shot.

"Take the young and the strong, gather all the weapons you can from the homes!" Alpha shouted to Cherno.

Suddenly Momar, Alpha's oldest son, came racing toward them. "Father!" he shouted, "it is the coming of the antichrist!"

"No my son, only the coming of the devils. Take a rifle and gather the old men, the women and the children, you must lead them on the path out of town away from the river. There is no time to take anything. Guide them to the waterfall at the stream. They should be safe there. I will send word for you. If you do not hear from me within the hour, continue east eight miles to Fanaay, it is a good village of Muslims, they will shelter…"

Before Alpha could finish, more cannon fire rocked the compound leveling the huts next to them. "Go!" he shouted to his son.

"Cherno, we must be prepared to fight. They will send men." Alpha turned to look about him and already there were nearly a hundred of Jamtan's men filing into its little market. Most were armed with only lances or bows, or daggers. A few had old muskets of rifles that had only been used for hunting. He and Cherno began organizing them and together they charged toward the banks of the river where the white, brown, and black men were firing from defensive positions behind the ruins of the mosque and the neighboring homes. These were the first white men ever to set foot on this part of God's green earth.

Fire engulfed everything, the women and children were screaming and running for the edges of the town. Bullets ripped through the air as did the rhythmic explosion of cannon shots. The bleating of the lambs was deafening. As Alpha charged to defend his place of peace by breaking his oath never again to kill any child of Adam, two thoughts raced through his mind. *Where are the rest of my children? And where is Zamar?*

☪

Everything in Zamar's life had been leading up to this morning, but nothing had prepared her for it. The scene that began the day was eerily familiar. She awoke to see the hideous angular grey form of her father, Sultan

Nazreel standing over her. Again they were alone in a cave, and again it was an ominous visit. He looked much as he always had, stroking his long copper-colored beard and snarling words at her through his fangs. But this time she saw age, weariness, and something else hiding behind his hateful eyes.

"Well, Zamar," Nazreel boomed, "it certainly has taken me quite a while to find you. It has taken the better part of an hour to find this place, not to mention the thirty years since you disappeared."

Zamar's heart sank as she realized that this was no nightmare. Dawn had just broken, and the cave was still very dark, but her father really was standing before her in the midst of her haven of peace behind the waterfall. All of her childhood fear, sadness, and longing came rushing back to her. She drove them away, and stood to face him as she knew she should have done long ago.

Here in this place, where she had wed and raised a family, she would not feel like a helpless child. Here she would be herself. She rose from her bed and stood face to face with her father. The four-foot tall coal black jinniya with copper eyes and mane now stood just a bit taller than her much wider and bulkier father, and she looked down at him as she spoke.

"Why have you come here?" Zamar boomed back at him, deepening her voice to match his and staring unblinkingly into his eyes.

"Do not play tricks with me child!" Nazreel said, his voice coming from everywhere all at once. "I am not impressed!"

"This is my home!" Zamar bellowed, with reverberations that lingered long after the words. The fixtures on the bed rattled, its sheets ruffled, and dust tumbled from the ceiling of the cave. Zamar did not break her father's gaze, but she waited until the dust had settled before she spoke again. "You are an uninvited guest here! I will speak as I please!" With these words, a hot breeze swirled through the room lifting Nazreel's beard from the ground, almost knocking him off balance.

"So be it, child," Nazreel said in his ordinary voice, "I have only come to talk," he said as his lipless mouth curled into an eerie grin.

"What do you wish to discuss?" Zamar said coolly and impatiently, but without causing a tremor inside the cave. "I have come to discuss the terms of your surrender," Nazreel growled. "You will submit to arrest and you will face trial for your crimes. This is the only hope that you have of not receiving the death penalty. If you surrender willingly, you will only face life imprisonment. If we must take you by force, then you will surely be put through the most heinous torture and then put to death."

"This you would promise to your own daughter?" Zamar sighed, feeling once again her sense of loss welling inside her.

"I have no daughter!" Nazreel shouted. Then he lowered his voice and continued. "You will submit yourself to me now, and perhaps I will not be forced to take your fire!"

"I see," Zamar said, smiling. "I think I finally see. I never understood you until this very moment."

"What are you saying?" Nazreel muttered impatiently, "will you surrender or not?"

"I never understood," Zamar continued, "why you never loved me. But now I can finally see it in your eyes."

"Stop wasting time. This is…" Nazreel tried to speak but Zamar interrupted him.

"You see Nazreel," Zamar said, uttering her father's name for the first time in her life, "almost all of the most vicious heartless predators love their own children. But there are some that are incapable even of this. The male lions sometimes kill their own offspring because they are afraid of one day having to fight them for control of the pride. They kill them while they are still weak, because they know that a day is coming when the cub will be too strong."

"This is foolishness!" Nazreel said, "You are nothing more than a cowardly bookkeeper! Do you really think that…"

"Shut up you old monster!" Zamar bellowed, shaking the walls of the cave once more. "You never loved me. And you could never show any emotion around me at all, because the only feeling you ever felt when you looked at me was fear. Now you are too old and weak to hide it. All this time, I thought it was disappointment. But it was *fear*. You knew long ago that you had lost my love, and you worried that one day you would earn my hate. You always regretted saving my life, because you have always feared that one day I would come for you and take your pride!"

"Enough of this nonsense," Nazreel boomed. "Face trial for your crimes and you may spend the rest of your days in prison, otherwise you will be extinguished."

"Tell me, *Nazreel*," Zamar said, now dripping with contempt, "where is this prison that can hold me? How will you take my flame when *I*, unlike *you*, am impervious to iron and salt?"

Nazreel glanced upward furtively, searching with his eyes for the narrow hole near the top of the cave. "We know that you have been protecting the fleshling and his village," he said nervously. "We are sure that he is the one. Our own seers have seen his face written in the sands. There is nothing you can do now to save him…"

"What?!" Zamar shuddered as she began to understand. "That's what this is all about? Alpha?"

Nazreel began to hover above the ground as if he was about to fly away. Zamar reached out with her left hand and grabbed her father by the wrist. Then with her right hand, she reached out toward the frame of the bed, and pulled one of its iron beams from its moorings. With a simple effort of will, she heated the beam and bent it, wrapping it around Nazreel's neck. "You are not going anywhere!" she shouted.

Nazreel screeched in pain as his head and shoulders hardened into solid rock.

"Where is Alpha?" Zamar screamed so loudly that pebbles began to tumble from the ceiling above them."

Nazreel look up again toward the hole in the ceiling, but this time he screamed, "Now! Now! Before it's too late! She's going to kill me!"

☾

Suddenly an endless stream of ethereal bodies came flowing through the narrow hole at the roof of the cave. A wall of wind whipped through the mouth of the waterfall. In an instant, the once peaceful cave was filled with three hundred jinn of all shapes and sizes. Zamar was momentarily surprised and let go of the iron bar that held her father in place. He staggered away from her, still part rock and part flame, before tumbling to the ground near the back of the cave.

These hundreds of jinn formed a circle around Zamar in the middle of the room. They arranged themselves in ranks, with some hovering above her so that she was completely surrounded in every direction. They covered her entirely, like a dome of smokeless fire.

Scores of jinn whirled about her. On Nazreel's command they began raining down beams of fire from their hands, swinging lashes of energy from the tips of their limbs, and screaming like banshees, filling the cavern with a deafening sound. The pulses of energy battered Zamar's body, staggering her repeatedly. When she was stunned, teams of jinn descended upon her and battered her with their enormous fists.

After a few moments of this Zamar had taken enough. She pulled apart the remaining beams of the bed at the center of the room and took two of them in her hands. The jinn that filled the cave gasped in terror as she melted the beams of iron with her fire and smoothed them into blades between her fingers. Finally she dipped them in the basin of water that sat beside the bed. Peals of steam bubbled from the clay pot. When a team of a dozen jinn rushed her, she swung one of the still warm blades and took their heads clean off.

Suddenly Zamar became a whirlwind, her hands whipping the blades in every direction, carving the jinn that surrounded her to ribbons. As the blades cut through them, their bodies first hardened, then shattered. They tried to flee screaming, but the jet black jinniya moved with shocking speed, appearing to be in every corner of the cave at once. After a few moments the screaming stopped. The room was filled with mounds of dust and rubble.

Nazreel was still in the corner with an iron beam wrapped around his neck. His whimpers of pain had turned into sobs of despair as he had watched Zamar carve three hundred of his mightiest jinn warriors into shards in less than a minute.

Zamar turned to him with a wild and ruthless look in her eyes. "WHERE IS ALPHA!?" she wailed. In that moment, the mounds of rubble in the room crumbled to a fine powder.

"I…will…tell you nothing," Nazreel stammered with all the defiance he could muster.

"Then I will deal with you later," Zamar said, and she flew through the hole in the roof of the cave.

☪

When she emerged into the half-light of the dawn, Zamar daughter of Nazreel saw sights that she had never before seen in her life. Against the waking blue-black sky she saw the silhouette of awful things. These beasts were made of smokeless fire. They could not be seen by the eyes of men and they did not cast a shadow, but they cast a pall over Zamar's eyes.

First were the winged beasts. Hundreds and hundreds of them filled the sky. When Zamar first saw them she did not know why they looked so strangely familiar. Then it struck her; It was the eyes. They all had those same cold lizard eyes that she had once known and hated.

"My God!" she cried out loud. "Can it be that Nemacus has bred himself with dragons?" Not only dragons. The sky was also filled with half-breed eagles, vultures, condors, and hawks.

As she lowered her gaze she realized that below them tens of thousands of jinn soldiers were hovering in ranks. As Zamar emerged from the cave, they assumed attack position. Everywhere she looked they covered the horizon. Along with the unholy beasts that filled the sky above her, they formed an impermeable wall keeping her from flying to Jamtan to find Alpha, to find her children.

Then Zamar looked at the plateau surrounding her. Hundreds of bounty hunters had her completely encircled. These elementals could not fly, but she knew that they too were impervious to iron and would be almost impossible to kill. Nearly all of them were mounted upon beasts.

As she studied the monsters, Zamar realized an awful truth. Nemacus had not only copulated with dragons and birds, but with every sort of predator that crawled on four legs. *The beasts too will die hard*, she thought, *if they are only half-jinn then iron will not destroy them.*

He must have committed thousands of acts of bestiality trying to bring about the perfect army of jinn-animal hybrids! She thought. Nemacus' pale and scaly skin covered the airy bodies of what otherwise would have been cheetahs, hyenas, jackals, and lions. These creatures were mangled and grotesque. They had lizard-like eyes in places where they did not belong. They had forked slits for tongues. They had scales and mange where fur ought to have been. And then there were the elephants. Some of these mammoth beasts had tusks of fire emerging from the middle of their foreheads, like monstrous misshapen unicorns. Before Zamar knew what had happened, they were all closing in on her with murderous haste. She said a prayer as the sky turned black around her and the hybrid beasts descended upon her.

☾

The dawn had not yet broken, but light was filling the sky. Momar was running, back and forth among rows of the young, old, and weak, spurring them on toward the waterfall as his father had commanded. They had been scrambling over the uneven ground for nearly half of an hour when they reached the waterfall in the stream. But as Momar jogged ahead of the pack of more than a hundred of the people of Jamtan, he realized right away that they could not stop here as his father had instructed.

The sun had not yet risen, but everywhere he looked the light of dawn was bringing streaks of bright blue to chase the blackness from the sky. Everywhere, that is, except in the sky above the waterfall. As he approached, Momar saw what could only be described as a tornado, or rather many tornadoes, with sand, dust, and debris whirling in every direction, darkening the sky. Alternating gusts of freezing cold and blistering hot air brushed over his body as he approached. Instinctively, he said a prayer of protection and clutched the talismans that were tied to his left shoulder.

"We cannot stop here!" the boy shouted. "We must continue on to the next village. It will be two hours walk or more."

Sokhna, out of breath and with terrible pains shooting through her stomach, doubled over to catch her breath. She had only found one of her children, Momar, in the crowd that had escaped the village. In spite of her fear for her children that remained at the village, in spite of the agonizing pain that ripped through her insides, she looked at her son with pride, realizing that he was becoming a man before her eyes. It was the last thought she had before she blacked out in a shallow trench, as the pain in her gut overwhelmed her. No one had seen her fall.

Then one of Assan's wives began screaming. She was the one that had lain in the mud on the riverbank in a prior exodus nine years before. She had seen the Cheddo disappear and she had watched Alpha Ba walk across the water. Now she began to wipe tears away from her face and shout at his son. "No! We must go back. My co-wife is not here, my husband is not here! My children…We must return for them! You are only a child yourself, you do not understand!"

Momar's hands were shaking like leaves on the rifle his father had handed to him, but he made his voice as deep and loud as he could before he responded. Even over the whipping sounds of the sandstorm that raged above them, he shouted loud enough for all to hear:

"I am Momar, son of Alpha Ba! He has commanded me to lead you and he has commanded you to follow! I will not have the blood of those he entrusted to me on my hands. No one is going back! No one will even look back! We will run at speed to the next village, we will warn them of the coming of the whites, and we will pray that God will reunite us with our families, whether in this world or the next!"

☪

Back in Jamtan, the world was coming to an end. Half of the houses in the village were burning. Their thatched roofs went up like one bonfire after the next. Explosions of Greek Fire rocked the town. Some of the women and children who hid in their huts waiting for the madness to end were cooked alive. Others were crushed by cannonballs. A few had managed to hide under beds or overturned horse carts, preventing them from being crushed by the crumbling walls of a village that would not live to see another day.

The crew of the *Jezebel* had fanned out from the banks of the river enclosing Jamtan in a semi-circle. They were armed to the teeth with the finest European tools of death. When the men of Jamtan rushed their attackers with lances and machetes, Nemacus' brigade of one hundred jinn soldiers blew hot sand and dust in their eyes. The slavers then served them with a hail of bullets.

They enclosed the village, little by little, choking it. Nemacus' jinn flew in and out of the bodies of the *Jezebel*'s crew. They urged them on, calling them to bravery, and valor through merciless dismemberment of the bodies of the dead. They urged them to disobey O'Meara's orders and to kill as many as they could, to violate any isolated women they found in the rubble whether young or old.

Some of the jinn even tried to possess the men of Jamtan and use them as weapons against their brothers, but they found it impossible to penetrate them. Everyone that lived in this village wore talismans written and sealed by Alpha Ba himself.

This protection shielded them from possession, but it could not reinforce their bones, nor harden their soft and weak flesh. The bodies of the believers broke, burned, and bled. Within an hour the slavers had the village under control, half a hundred of Jamtan's ablest men lay dead in the streets, and the little village of peace had spent nearly all of its meager munitions.

☾

The governor of the City of the Whites, patted the heads of his two German shepherds as he put his foot down on the muddy banks of Jamtan. Climbing up the shallow bank, he took in the sunrise, lit his cigar, and began walking among his officers speaking rapidly. The crew of the *Jezebel* was already marching rows of captives toward the Governor for inspection. Their hands were tied behinds their backs, and they were tied together by the neck in groups of six. After a few moments and much commotion, one of O'Meara's black henchmen, the one holding the dogs at the end of two thick ropes, began to speak to the people in a very broken version of the language of the people of Futa, along with much Wolof. Few of the people that could hear him understood all of the words, but everyone understood the meaning.

"You come out now! Lower your swords! Release your guns! No more blood is needed. You are all slaves now. But you will live. O-May-ra and the white men do not eat blacks. This is a lie told to scare children. You come out now! Lower your guns! Release your swords! No more blood is needed!"

☪

Alpha and Cherno crouched together beneath an overturned canoe some fifty yards away from where O'Meara had come aground. In the dark and commotion, none of the *Jezebel's* crew had seen them slip through the brush near the riverbank and crawl under an old, broken, and dusty canoe that had sat unused next to the river for almost four months.

From this sheltered position behind the enemy's advancing lines, Cherno, who was the village's best marksman, had shot four of O'Meara's men in the back without being detected. In the early dawn and with the cannons blasting, Cherno had been able to fire undetected.

But now he was almost out of ammunition. Aside from a single musket ball, the only arms they had left were two machetes and Alpha's silver dagger.

"We must surrender," Alpha whispered to Cherno.

"No!" Cherno hissed quietly. "My teacher, we cannot. I would rather die as a man than live as a slave!"

"I know Cherno," Alpha replied, "You are brave. But if we continue to fight, more of God's people will die awful deaths here today."

"They will be martyrs," Cherno replied, using the Arabic word.

"They are already martyrs. We that have suffered what has happened here today are all *witnesses*," Alpha whispered, using the word from the tongue of Futa. "But the children of Adam are the most precious of God's creations," Alpha continued, "any believer that can stop their blood from being spilt without reason is obliged to do so."

"Master," Cherno pleaded, "our people will never surrender to these animals. They will do awful things to us. Awful things to our women." Cherno looked up and saw his betrothed, Jeneba, being marched before the fat white man with the cigar. Even at this distance he could see him smiling widely. "We must do something!"

"There may be one thing left," Alpha whispered solemnly. "Cut off the head and the body will no longer be able to fight."

"Yes," Cherno nodded, "I think I understand. Master, let me shoot the fat, red-eared white man!"

"No, my son," Alpha replied, "You only have one shot left. And until they release those dogs, the element of surprise will be with us. No one needs to know where you are. You must stay concealed here. I will need you to fire that shot when the time is right. After you shoot, do not wait to see what happens. Disappear into the river and swim as far away from here as you can. Trust that I will cut the head off the snake with my own right hand."

☪

Alpha, son of Amadu had never killed anyone. He took a deep breath and closed his eyes. He said a prayer of peace on the Prophet and remembered that the Prophet had never raised his hand against a human being until he raised his sword to keep the Muslims from being exterminated. He knew that now a sacrifice was demanded of him as well.

In his mind he saw before him the kind face of the Arab stranger that had smiled at him in the mosque. He smiled back at him and a tear rolled down his right cheek as he understood the gift that he had been given. With his eyes still closed, he saw the faces of his children, first Khadija and Momar, Khalifa and Mariama. Then Tamsir and Echo, Samba and Demba, Whisper and Hush. Next, his thoughts turned to Sokhna and Zamar: *I must leave this place today not knowing whether they are alive or dead.*

Hearing these words in his mind, Alpha thought of those who had gone before him. He thought of his brother Samba, and his father and mother Amadu and Ayssatu. He could see their smiling faces, and the flowers that grew on their graves back in his homeland.

"All thanks are for God," he whispered, "Lord of the Worlds. The Compassionate and the Merciful. For Him is the Kingdom, For Him the Praises, and His Decree is written upon each and every thing."

Finally, Alpha Ba looked outward upon the world again. Tears were pouring from Cherno's eyes. The young man had not set eyes on his own father in more than nine years, and he knew that today he was gazing for the last time upon the man who had been his father ever since.

Alpha smiled at Cherno and spoke. "Every breath drawn by the children of Adama and Hawa is a priceless gift that can never be repaid. God was alone in His perfection for an eternity before He made the Heavens and the Earth. We did nothing to deserve all of the splendor He has blessed us with. And God alone will never taste death. *Everything is perishing except His Face.* From Him we come and to Him we shall return."

☪

"Bismillah," Alpha whispered, as he crawled out from beneath the canoe on his belly. He managed to make it to the line of brush undetected. Momentarily safe behind the bushes, Alpha surveyed the situation. The fat white man stood up from the bank of the river, still no more than fifty yards away. *There is something strange about him*, Alpha thought, before turning his attention to the four men that were guarding him.

Standing within ten paces of this fat man were four killers, two white and two black. All were carrying pistols and rifles, and one held the dogs at the end of a leash. *Killing their leader will be easy,* Alpha thought. *He is not even armed. I can cover the ground between us in five beats of a drum, but before I count to three, the others will have shot me dead. I need to steal two seconds from them.*

Almost as he thought it, two shots rang out from somewhere near the village market, everyone turned at once to look, and most of the mercenaries began running toward the market. The man with the dogs went running alongside them, and made a sound and a gesture spurring the beasts on to find the source of the trouble.

Alpha Ba sprang into action. His feet carried him over the hard-packed earth with blinding speed. Pain burned in his legs so hard did he run. Between him and O'Meara there was a very tall red-haired white man armed with a pistol. At the sound of the shots, he had begun to jog towards the market, but now he saw and heard something charging at him from his right. He spun about with his pistol drawn and cocked the hammer as Alpha closed in.

Alpha's body called up old memories from his days as a young wrestler. Black David, the Small Axe of Futa, chopped down this towering man with a single blow. Alpha slid to the ground from a dead run and kicked the man in the knee, instantly shattering the bones and tearing the ligaments. The man fell to the ground screaming. As he did, the black man standing a few feet away aimed his pistol. Alpha somersaulted away as the shot sped past him. When the black man reached in his waistband for his other gun, Alpha pounced upon him like a cat. The two were now locked in hand- to-hand combat.

The other mercenaries all began running back to the riverbank, but mercifully they were not in range for a clear shot, and the dogs were nowhere in sight. Only the one remaining white bodyguard had a shot, and he dared not take it.

Alpha was intertwined with his comrade and they were moving about so quickly and struggling so violently that he could not get a clean shot. Normally, this white officer, Lieutenant Davies, would not have hesitated to take two shots and kill both negroes just to be sure. But unbeknownst to all but O'Meara, who had long been blackmailing him, Davies was *attached* to this black man. The man locked in life and death struggle with Alpha had been Davies' slave and manservant since the black man was little more than a boy.

Many years ago, he had bought the thirteen-year old in Senegal and taken him away to the Gold Coast where he was stationed. Davies spoke sweetly to the youth, whom he renamed Nero. Jameson Davies fed Nero meat, cakes, and wine. He caressed his head, called him a clever boy, and taught him to speak—and even read—a little bit of English. He promised repeatedly that he would never hurt him.

After two months of this, he finally broke his promise. After a night of drinking wine and reading lewd stories, Nero awoke chained to his master's bed. The boy sobbed and wailed as his owner and only friend molested him repeatedly. Davies continued with such molestations for months until finally the boy's resistance broke. They had secretly been lovers ever since. Davies had long promised to free Nero, but he never had, and he never would.

☪

From the scars purposefully cut along his temples and from the way he countered his every move, Alpha surmised that this creature must have once learned the ways of the people of Futa. In another life, this *devil*, had probably been a *boy* much like he was. Instantly, Alpha realized how he would subdue him. Without really thinking of it consciously, he recalled a foreign technique that he had once seen in a match between a man from Jolof and a Sereer giant from the lands to the south. The Jolof-Jolof had gone limp for the briefest of moments, and then used his opponent's aggressiveness against him. That night, Alpha had practiced the move again and again with Samba, and later he had used it against his most skilled opponents.

Alpha Ba relaxed his every limb. For a brief moment, Nero supported his weight for him, then the slaver instinctively rocked his own weight backward to prepare a vicious blow. When Alpha felt his adversary lean back, he wrapped his left leg around Nero's right, and pushed on the man's torso with all his might. Nero toppled over onto his back. As Alpha fell on top of him, he cushioned his own fall with his right hand, while cocking back his left fist. With it he delivered a crushing blow to the right side of Nero's face just as the slave's head hit the ground. With his head braced against the earth, the blow landed flush. The face of Davies' beloved venereal toy collapsed entirely. Blood and teeth poured from him.

James Davies had his pistol trained on Alpha but he was so shocked to see his lover mangled and disfigured that he hesitated momentarily. From his concealed position, Cherno fired his one remaining shot. It split Lieutenant Davies' head, leaving Alpha with nothing between himself and the fat white man except ten yard's of God's wide-open earth.

☪

Alpha locked eyes with the man. For the briefest of moments, he saw something behind the man's eyes. It was something ancient and familiar, a thing teeming with hatred and contempt. Whatever it was, it made the hairs on the back of Alpha's neck stand on end.

Then, in less than an instant, the light went out of the man's eyes, Nemacus had flown out of him. Alpha did not see the devilish jinn go, but he saw the change in the man. All that remained in those eyes now was fear and cowardice.

O'Meara broke Alpha's gaze and turned to run. He scrambled towards his soldiers as they continued to stream toward the banks of the river. "Shoot him!" he screamed, "Shoot that nigger now!"

A dozen shots rang out. One ripped through Alpha's left shoulder, but he hardly felt it. He was within two steps of this whale and he was not going to let it out of his net. Alpha reached into his waistband with his right hand and pulled out the silver knife that his wife had given him nine years ago in the hidden mystery of her desert cave of wonders. He leapt atop O'Meara, and grabbed the man around the neck with his left arm.

The excruciating pain Alpha Ba felt nearly blinded him. The ball lodged in his left shoulder had torn through his sinews and rent his ligaments. His left hand was broken in three places from crushing the face of Nero the Sodomist

Slave. Still, he collared the impudent red-faced man, who had not yet even dropped his cigar. It fell in the mud only as Alpha reached across to the front of the man with his right hand. With all the force he could muster, he plunged the silver knife into O'Meara's lungs. At this the bloated beast gasped, and began choking on his own blood.

Alpha had never killed a man, so he did not realize that O'Meara was already dying. He spun him around so that he could see his face to be sure. His ears and nose were covered with rosacea. His lips moved, but they made no sound, except for a kind of gurgling as blood filled his lungs. Alpha looked into his eyes and saw both his own reflection and Azra'il the Angel of Death over his own shoulder.

O'Meara cringed with terror. At this moment, Alpha plunged the knife through the fat on the left side of the white man's chest, puncturing his heart. *O-May-ra*, the one whose name was used to scare children, was on his way to the Fire.

☪

Alpha's ears were filled with the sounds of gunshots coming from behind him—more shots than could be counted. He was facing the Senegal River. He looked up and saw the spot that he had seen in his dreams ten years ago. It was the place where the words *Jam Tan* had been written in the sand and on the water. He saw the spot where he had wrestled the lion, and where he had met his wife.

"Alhamdulillah, peace only," were his last words as the bullets riddled his back. With his dying vision, Alpha Ba saw the Ka'aba, the House of God, rising from the waters of the river. He had seen its reflection in his washbasin yesterday, and now he knew why. He was going to God, he was going to Peace, he was going Home.

☪

Zamar daugher of Nazreel moved with blinding speed, dealing death to the army of jinn and half-caste monsters that assailed her. She was too busy to feel the twinge in her heart as her beloved husband took leave of the world. She too was fighting for her life. With her iron blades she was cutting jinn into piles of dust, but her metal weapons passed right through the half-breed beasts and bounty hunters.

The latter kept lashing her with the cords of energy that they used to bind their prey among the jinn. Zamar was not like the ordinary criminals they pursued. She could not be contained by these cords of warped flame. But they did lash her body, causing her searing pain. Moreover, when the hybrids or their ropes touched her, she could not change form. She could neither expand nor contract, nor could she become a true wind.

Each time she tried to fly away to Jamtan to rescue her husband, the flying demons and dragons contained her, attacking with their beaks and claws. She was far stronger than they, but she could not kill them easily with iron. She had to beat them to death one by one. Her fists and feet moved with deadly speed and precision, but she had been struggling for two hours now and she had barely killed half of the unholy army. She began to wonder how much longer she could fight like this. *Perhaps my father will take my fire after all*, she thought.

Suddenly Zamar was struck with inspiration. Thinking of her father reminded her of something she had read long ago in his scrolls. She could see the words in front of her as though they were still on the page.

The Elementals grow from the seed of fire planted in a womb of clay. They follow their fathers and live in the world of the fiery, unseen by the creatures of mud. Like the mudballs they fear neither iron nor salt. Like the mudballs they have a weightiness to them. They are bound to their mother, the earth, and they cannot fly. They must walk on two legs like fleshlings, and they cannot enter the bodies of the their cousins, the Adamites.

It was this last part that grabbed Zamar's attention. *They cannot enter the children of Adam,* she thought, *but can they be entered?* Zamar looked into the eyes of one of the bounty hunters as it lashed her with its ropes. She shook herself free from his lashes for the briefest second and flew right into his mouth. Immediately he doubled over in pain. After a second, his man-like eyes began to grow wider and wider. Suddenly, the bounty hunter exploded, sending shock waves everywhere. The explosion alone killed a half-dozen of his fellow mercenaries, and it fatally wounded the hybrid beasts on which they were mounted. Where the bounty hunter had stood, there was now only the airy figure of Zamar, four-foot tall and coal black, pulsing with the brightest of flames.

Zamar now had a weapon. One by one, Zamar the Scribe, who had refused to be a wearer of human *men*, entered into the hybrid offspring of human *women*. One explosion after the next rocked the unseen world. All along the plateau above the waterfall, bounty hunters and four-legged brutes were exploding like bombs, releasing shockwaves of energy.

Within minutes Zamar had killed every last one of the hundreds of bounty hunters that had been sent to pursue her. She immediately tried to make her escape toward Jamtan, but the flying jinn had orders to delay her as long as possible. They descended upon her a thousand at a time, clawing, biting, and pounding upon her fiery body. This was suicide. Zamar retrieved her iron blades and dismembered the jinn twenty and thirty at a time. The faster they flew at her, the more quickly she sent them to their deaths.

On the valley floor below Sokhna heard only a roaring, deafening wind. Sand and dust flew everywhere, so much that she could hardly open her eyes. When she managed to squint enough to see the cloud, all she could tell was that it blocked out the sun, and that dust whirled in every direction. Her insides were throbbing. Tears welled in her eyes and mixed with the dust to cement them shut.

Every now and again she rubbed them clean and looked up at the ominous dust cloud. She was almost sure that she saw birds flying through it.

☪

Dust and debris littered the plain. The jinn were dead. The elementals were dead. Their crawling hybrid beasts were dead. Only the flying monsters barred Zamar's path to her husband now. *How is it that they fly?* Zamar wondered. *The books say that the Elementals are bound to their mother the Earth.* Then Zamar understood: *These things can fly because these are flying things. They fly not because they are part jinn, but because they have wings. I shall cripple their wings once and for all. I shall ground them so that they never fly again.*

Zamar flew right into the crowd of dragons and devil-birds. They beat their wings as quickly as they could to chase her as she sped upwards. They clung to her and clawed at her. They slowed—but did not stop—her ascent. She climbed higher and higher as they lashed at her with their fiery talons and tusks. They would not let go, but many of them began to fade and flicker as they reached the top of the sky. Such things, it seemed, were never meant to fly so high. The air was thin and light and even though she was being mauled by some of the most awful things in creation, Zamar savored her momentary nearness to the heavens.

Then she began diving to earth. The creatures that clung to her arms and to one another writhed as they struggled to maintain their grasp. The velocity was unspeakable. The earth, which had, for a moment been a rounded sphere quickly became an endless flat plain below them. At first it was featureless. Then its hills and valleys rapidly came back into sight. Zamar could now see the stream and the waterfall below approaching. She propelled herself headlong towards the narrow hole at the top of the cave where her father, Nazreel, was still trapped in an iron noose.

Hundreds of beasts now clung to her arms and to one another. They trailed behind her like the tails of two comets, or rather like two giant gnarled wings. As she neared the ground, Zamar exerted an extraordinary effort of will. Just before she crashed into the surface she stopped herself with an abrupt somersault that left her head facing up and her feet pointing down. The grotesque birds that clung to her arms could not stop their inexorable momentum, and Zamar whipped her arms toward the ground with all her furious might, freeing herself from their grasp, and slamming the monsters against the plateau. They exploded on contact shattering the midday silence with what sounded like peals of thunder.

☾

Sokhna was passed out on the floor of the valley, not far from the stream, the waterfall, and the mouth of the cave. She startled at what she feared was another cannonball crashing through the wall of her hut. She struggled to gather herself through the stupor induced by her pain, fatigue, and grief. She looked up for the source of the sound and saw that the plateau above the waterfall was crumbling. Rubble was everywhere. The falls, which had flown directly over the rocks from the plateau above, now appeared to wash out a large cavern that had been hidden from sight. Massive amounts of rock and dust flowed into the stream turning it brown. But visible in the brown soup that poured into the stream were scraps of metal and cloth. Sokhna raised her head to see into the stream that flowed not far from where she lay. There she saw leather books, sheets of paper, and whole pieces of fruit pouring out of the cavern and into the stream.

Sokhna rubbed her eyes as if she did not trust them. When she opened them again, she saw a small, black, catlike creature standing before her on two legs. She screamed and tried to get up to run, but the pain in her belly was so excruciating that she could not. She covered her head, and began begging not to be eaten.

Zamar was spent. She felt far too weak to try to take and hold human form. She stood before Sokhna now as herself. *Perhaps I should have come to her this way long ago*, she thought.

Sokhna shrieked again, but when she peeked through her fingers expecting to see the beast's teeth and lips closing in, she saw the thing leaning against a rock instead, exhausted. In spite of her fear, Sokhna studied its face.

"Oh my God!," she exclaimed. "Zamar, is that you?"

"Yes, my co-wife," she sighed. "This is me as I am."

"I don't understand," Sokhna said. "How can this be?"

"My sister," Zamar whispered solemnly, "can it be that you never guessed that I was a jinniya?"

Sokhna winced as pains shot through her gut. "Seeing you like this now," she replied, "I feel like I must have always known. But the pain in my body is proof that I did not."

"Now *I* am the one who does not understand," Zamar said.

"It is all my fault," Sokhna cried, the tears beginning to fall down her cheeks. "The Old Witch tricked me, but it is all my fault."

"Sokhna," Zamar said in a hushed tone, "speak plainly."

"I am sorry Zamar. I am so very sorry for all of it. I was the witch from the very beginning. I hated you, though you had done nothing to harm me."

"My sister, I forgive you," Zamar whispered. "Do not worry. I never took any harm from it."

"No. You still do not understand. I put a spell on you. The old hag told me that I could curse the fruit of your womb. She said that once you were barren, Alpha would love me again. *Only me.* Now I see, she did not know you were a jinniya. It is as it should be. This curse has planted itself inside me instead. Something awful is happening to me. I can feel it. My womb is turning to stone."

Zamar reached out and touched Sokhna for the first time in their lives. She placed her right hand on her belly and closed her eyes to try to envision the source of her co-wife's pain. "There is no god but God," Zamar exclaimed. In her mind's eye she could see it as clear as day. She saw a fetus, perhaps three months old, that had calcified in Sokhna's womb. Sokhna would carry this Sleeping Baby with her for the rest of her days as a reminder of her sin.

"You will live my sister," Zamar said, trying to smile. "But...I am...I am so sorry Sokhna, your child will not." Zamar said, choking on the words. "Did you not know that you were already pregnant?"

Sokhna's shoulders heaved and her nose ran as she sobbed uncontrollably. Her eyes nearly bled, so hard did she cry. Then she tried to compose herself. "I deserve this. May God forgive me. I invited wickedness and evil into our place of peace. I spilled blood in the name of demons. I do not even know what the words I said might mean. I only know that my sins have brought death and destruction to our village."

"Death and destruction?" Zamar asked, raising her voice with concern. "What do you mean? Sokhna why are you here alone? Where is Alpha? What do you mean a curse on my womb? Where are my children? Where are your children?"

"The white men came Zamar. They came before the roosters crowed and began throwing stones and fire at our homes. Many of the people were already dead when we ran. No more than one hundred of the weak, the women, and the children made it out. That was hours ago. Since then, the ones left behind have probably died or been taken as slaves. Of my children I have seen only Momar. I have not seen yours since last night. There is no telling what has become of them, or of Alpha…" Sokhna's voice broke off as the tears overcame her.

Zamar looked up and saw that the sun was near the top of the sky. *Have I really been fighting these monsters for half of a day?* She turned to fly, but she could not move. She looked up and realized that Sokhna was staring at her sadly.

"Look away now, Sokhna, and release me," Zamar said, "I will go and find our husband, and our children. God willing."

☪

Zamar sped toward Jamtan, but she was arriving hours too late. The fires still smoked, but the flames had long since burned out. Zamar surveyed the town and could not believe what she saw. The mosque was destroyed.

☪

Dozens of huts were burned. Then, as she landed at what used to be her bend of the river, she saw what used to be her husband. The body of Alpha Ba was lying face up in the mud near the bank of the river, covered in blood, with his eyes wide open as if they were staring into eternity. Zamar knew that it was him, but without the life in his eyes she could hardly recognize him. What made him *him* was the spirit that had lived within this body, not the robes of flesh and bone.

Zamar fell into her human body and knelt beside her husband. She kissed his lips and closed his eyes. She lingered there for a moment waiting for tears to come, but they did not. At this instant, Zamar felt nothing. There was only emptiness inside her. For a brief moment she wondered if she—like so many of her kind—was heartless.

She became a wind and blew through the town to Alpha's compound. Nothing stirred within it. She drifted to the hut where her children slept whenever they stayed the night in the village of men. It was charred and black. The melted iron bolts were all that was left of the door. Zamar descended into the hut taking her natural jinn form as she did. The first things she saw were the pebbles from the Wuri game; nothing else had survived the blaze intact.

Then she saw the six charred bodies. *Children's bodies*. She could not even recognize her own babies, so thoroughly had the Greek fire consumed their skins and cooked their flesh. But two of the bodies were very small, two were a little larger, and the last two were larger still. These had fallen where the door should have been. *Whisper, Hush, Samba, and Demba died in their sleep! Tamsir and Echo must have been awakened and tried to make a way out!*

Zamar was heartbroken. Now the feelings all came at once. She spun away from the hut and into one of the village's main lanes. She felt dizzy and weak, her flame flickered, and before she knew it, she had involuntarily fallen out of her jinn form. She staggered a few steps and fell to her knees. She tried to stand but she couldn't. Convulsions ripped through her. They started in her stomach and radiated up her torso, stiffening her neck, and sending her lurching forward.

The jinniya was vomiting for the first time, but there was nothing in her stomach. So for what felt like an eternity, Zamar was doubled over, moaning and heaving in the smoldering streets of Jamtan, stark naked in her human body. Tears poured from her eyes like rain, and she wailed and pounded her fists on the ground before sinking face-first into the dust.

☪

She did not know how long she had been laying this way when a voice roused her from this state somewhere between sleep and madness. "Peace be upon you," the voice called out.

Zamar turned about to see a tall slender jinn, whose face was branded with the mark of Sultan Nazreel's army. In spite of her anguish and exhaustion, she whirled into jinn form, raised her hands, and prepared to slay the soldier. But, then he spoke again.

"Peace be upon you Zamar daughter of Nazreel, and I beg that you do not take my flame until you have heard what I have to say."

"A curse be upon you," Zamar snarled. "Tell me why I should not send you to Hell right now, so you can rejoin the rest of your devilish brood. Sultan Nazreel is finished, and so is his army."

"You are right to have killed them, and you are right to wish me dead," the jinn sighed. "We came to your home unprovoked and disturbed you. Nemacus and his company helped the manhunters lay waste to the village that you have protected. You have been wronged by my kind. When I have spoken my peace, I will leave my life in your hands. But, I've resolved to tell you what I saw here today, and I swear to you that I had no part in it."

"This village that I have *protected*? You ignorant piece of filth," Zamar said, scowling. "Do none of you understand? He was my *husband*. These were my *children*," she cried, motioning toward the smoking ruins. My tie to this place was no jinn's territorial fetish. Those that died here were part of my light and my flame. A heartless demon such as you would know nothing of such things."

The jinn soldier scoffed and shook his head.

"Do you mock me?" Zamar shouted, raising her hand again.

"No…no…I do not mock you," the soldier stammered. "I meant no disrespect. It's just that now I understand why I am…here. I mean, why *you* are here. Why *we* are here, I suppose."

"Stop stammering like an idiot," Zamar growled, "or I will kill you just to shut you up."

At this the soldier laughed aloud, and Zamar slapped him to the ground. She leapt atop him and grabbed a partially burned wooden board that had a rusty iron nail in it. She held the board so that the nail was suspended between the eyes of the soldier. She was about to drive it home when he cried out.

"I am sorry! Don't kill me! I too have married one of them!"

"What?"

"That is why I laughed," the soldier responded. "I fell in love with a fleshling. That is what I meant when I said that I understood. I have kept her hidden from Nazreel, from Nemacus. She...she has borne me children."

At the word 'children', Zamar began to sob uncontrollably and she fell back off of the soldier. After a moment, she composed herself, and the two jinn were left sitting on the beaten earth in a dead village looking at one another. The soldier broke the silence.

"They call me Al-Hajj," he said. "Nemacus gave me that name himself almost four years ago. He thinks it is very funny, but I like the name. He said that I had begun acting so *holy*, as if I had made the pilgrimage to Mecca and thought that I was too good to go on killing. I had to pretend to laugh, but inside I was screaming, because I was sure that he had discovered the truth. Nearly six months before I had married a human woman in the land they call Saalum, and she had made me submit myself to God before she would marry me."

"Why didn't you just take her by force?" Zamar scoffed. "Isn't that what your kind does? Why not just take her while she slept, she would never have known the difference? Why not wear her husband as she copulates with him? Nemacus and his sort do this all the time!"

"She was a virgin," Al-Hajj replied. "She had no husband. And besides, I did not want to *take* her. I wanted her to *give* herself to me. She was so kind, and so sweet, and so beautiful. I did not want to ravage her in her dreams, to steal her treasures while she slept. I wanted to know what it was to be loved by a thing that was loved by God."

Zamar threw her head back and stared toward the heavens for a moment before looking back at the soldier. "Perhaps that is why He made all of us," she muttered beneath her breath. "What would be the point of loving a thing that did not know you, or could not *choose* to love you back?"

Zamar had barely spoken the words. "What did you say?" Al-Hajj asked.

"It's not important," the black jinniya responded. "Listen, Al-Hajj, I am sorry that I cursed you. I am sorry that I threatened you. You said that there was something that you wished to tell me."

☪

"I saw it all," the slender jinn began. "I was meant to accompany Nemacus' company to destroy the village, but I could not. My heart would not allow it. I fled and hid myself away in an anthill not far from here. At first I did not want to look. Nemacus was right about me; I cannot bear to watch the blood of the children of Adam spilled anymore. But when I heard the thunderclaps from the cannons I turned to look and could not look away. Fire and lead rained from the sky and the humans were crushed and burned like dry blades of grass."

Zamar winced.

"I am sorry," Al-Hajj said, "this you already know. What you cannot know is that when the one they called O-May-ra died, the manhunters were not sure what to do. They panicked. Some quarreled with others. Nemacus tried to incite them to massacre all the people left in the village, but the soldiers were too busy shackling the prisoners and arguing with one another. They did not know what would happen to them once people learned that the fat white man was dead. Some believed they would all become outlaws and wanted criminals. Some wanted to flee across the ocean right away in their boat. They could only agree on two things. First, there would be no massacre—they needed to sell captives not corpses. Second, they wanted to get away from this place and back to the city of the whites as quickly as possible. They tied up the people that were left alive and loaded them onto the boat as quickly as they could. Nemacus and his company went with them."

"Some of the villagers still live?" Zamar asked.

"*Many* of them still live!" Al-Hajj exclaimed.

"When did this happen?" Zamar asked.

Al-Hajj looked up at the sun and saw that it was just beginning to climb down from its perch at the top of the sky. "The sun had risen but was not yet halfway to its zenith. It could not have been more than six hours ago."

A cool resolve spread across Zamar's face. "I will free them. And I will take my vengeance!"

Al-Hajj nodded. "By God I should accompany you, Zamar, but I pray that you will give me leave instead. I am not as strong as you, but I do not fear death at the hands of the men or of Nemacus. I would be honored to die at your side. But if Nemacus finds me there, he will surely guess my secret if he has not already. I fear not for myself, but for my wife and children. Even at this hour I do not know if they are alive or dead."

Zamar glanced toward the hut of her children and lowered her head grimly before speaking: "Tell me, Al-Hajj, are you able to take human form?" she asked.

He nodded.

"Then you must provide me one service before I will release you."

"I was part of a terrible crime against you, and yet you spared my life. I and all of my seed will forever owe you a debt of honor. I am at your service." With these words Al-Hajj became a tall slender brown skinned man with pitch black eyes and no hair anywhere on his face, head, or body.

"Please find a shovel, and help me to bury my family," Zamar said solemnly.

☪

The grave of Alpha Ba and his six children is unmarked. It was dug in the firm soil some distance up from the riverbank. But eight days after it was dug, a hot mineral spring began to bubble up through the rocks only a few steps away. Long after his story was forgotten by the children of Adam, the people of Futa still came to this hot spring. They bathed in its waters, which always smell strangely sweet, like ambergris or musk. Even today people from neighboring villages claim that it is a fountain of youth, washing away illness and infirmity.

☪

Zamar raced along the river, tearing a wake right through the middle of it. She was completely spent and fueled only by resolve and rage. Those that did this to Alpha, *to her children*, would pay. Nemacus would pay. She would kill every jinn and man in the city of the whites if she had to. If she could not save Alpha, she would save his people. Her people. He had brought them to her bend of the river so that she could protect them, and she had one last chance to make good on her promise.

As Zamar flew to within sight of the sea, a strange feeling passed over her. She stared out at the vast expanse of deep blue sea and realized that in all her 170 years, she had never set eyes on the ocean. Her father's people sometimes came to the sea, but she recalled that as a child her father had forbidden her from going without permission. And here it was before her, dotted with ships. She did not know where to begin looking for the people of Jamtan. She had encountered only a handful of canoes on the river, no slaveships. There were several wooden ships in harbor on the land side of the island, and she could see a handful of others on the seaward side of the island as well.

Zamar flew low over the waves to the seaward side of the island, but at first glance, the ships anchored there seemed empty. She was now flying over the open sea. She thought of climbing into the sky to get a better vantage point, but she could not shake the feeling that something strange was happening, or about to happen. She thought of turning into an eagle so that she could better survey the situation and search for the villagers. That was the strange part; just the thought of becoming the eagle usually initiated the transformation, but this time, no matter how much she willed it, she could not change form at all.

Suddenly Zamar felt searing pain burning into her right ankle. She looked down and saw that something like an elephant's trunk was wrapped around her. Whatever restrained her was not made of flesh, but of fire. Something like a jinn had her in its grasp. She cut loose from it, but another like it gripped her. Now she could see dozens of ethereal creatures gathering around her under the surface. They had enormous heads and eyes, and their long wiry trunks reached in every direction like so many arms. Zamar broke free again and immediately began flying straight up in the air to get a better look. This proved to be difficult, since she felt strangely heavy, but she was able to fly three hundred feet above the surface and look down at the depths.

Zamar did not fully understand what she saw, but she saw it. Or rather she saw them. Hundreds and hundreds of squid, octopi, fish, giant eels, mermen, and other fiery sea beasts for which there are no names in English were teeming just below the surface. They extended their tentacles higher and higher trying to grab Zamar and pull her into the depths, but it seemed that they could not leave the waters to pursue her. In that instant she had an awful thought: *Perhaps there is more of the unseen world hidden in the depths of the seas than in the space between the heavens and the earth!*

Just then something massive leapt from the water and threw itself high into the air. Zamar had never seen a thing made of flesh that was even half as large as this giant fish. It was facing away from her and she could see its large white underbelly. A few seconds later it leapt again, and Zamar could see the wraithlike form of some dark blue jinn riding upon its back!

Instinctively, Zamar wanted to climb higher in the sky to get herself clear of whatever else— whether of flesh or fire—might spring forth from the depths. She tried again to become the eagle, but to no avail. In her natural form she began to fly upwards, but she was now unbearably heavy. It was as if something invisible had tethered her to the bottom of the sea. She labored painfully to rise another hundred feet, then another, then another. She was exhausted.

Then she saw the eyes. Buried in the depths were a pair of enormous unblinking eyes. *I cannot believe I did not see them before! Maybe I was flying too low,* Zamar thought.

The giant eyes filled Zamar with a kind of primordial dread. They were ancient and awful, and they stared up at her from the depths. She was terrified, but she could not look away. *It is these eyes that keep me from changing form*, she thought. *What is down there?*

Then she remembered a thing long forgotten. As a child she had once asked her father's permission to go to the sea. He had replied with an answer that she was only now beginning to understand: "I did not mean that you need to ask my permission, Zamar, you need to ask permission of the *sea*. None of the jinn of the west come to it without asking permission from its master." Zamar had sometimes heard the children of Adam speak of the thing that lived in this part of the sea. They called her Maam Kumba.

The fishermen made burnt offerings to Maam Kumba before they went out in their canoes. Anytime someone drowned, some said that so-and-so was a sacrifice to Maam Kumba. Some of the people—even among those who called themselves Muslims—slaughtered animals on the beach in her name and threw them into the sea for her. Others dumped baskets of cowry shells and asked Maam Kumba to make them multiply. Sailors threw gold coins in the waters and asked Maam Kumba to bless their voyages, and when they survived a shipwreck, they gave her thanks. Some who called themselves Christians, believed that Maam Kumba was the Virgin Mary watching over them.

Whatever Maam Kumba was, she was certainly no innocent virgin, nor had she ever been anything like a human woman. She could be called a jinn only because there is no other word that better describes her. The only thing certain is that God made this ancient being for reasons known best to Him. Maam Kumba had been lurking in those depths for ages before the children of Adam walked the earth. When the giant brute lizards crawled on the land and swam in the seas, Maam Kumba was awake in the depths watching, and *eating*. But she was older than this. She swam in these seas before they were seas. She found this place when the Earth was still young

and she never left it. When the first rains had fallen to fill
the oceans, they fell upon her. When the Angels warred
against the rebel jinn before the time of Adam, she hid deep
in these depths and closed her eyes. And when the Shaitan
plummeted to earth, she opened them again.

On this day Zamar had discovered the extent of her
might, and on this day she would discover anew the extent
of her weakness. Though she had slaughtered a whole army
of jinn and beasts and ended half a millennium of rule by
Sultan Nazreel, Zamar was no match for the ancient evil
that resided in these depths. As she stared into those eyes
she knew this. When she closed her eyes to break the gaze
she found that she could still see Maam Kumba's eyes as if
they were engraved onto her eyelids.

When she opened them again to make the eyes go
away, she saw another unspeakable thing. Giant ghastly fish
were flying toward her. She knew of fish like these. The
people in these lands called them the lions of the sea, and
the books of knowledge called them sharks. But unlike the
sharks in the world of men, these were winged. Zamar was
heavy and could barely fly. She had no iron with which to
attack them. She did not even know if weapons of metal
would work against such monsters of the deep.

☾

A being as old as Maam Kumba counts centuries the way that the children of Adam count minutes. Little in the passing of the world disturbs such a creature. But for whatever reason—perhaps at the command of the Shaitan himself—Maam Kumba had taken deadly interest in this little pitch-black jinniya with the copper mane.

Zamar looked toward the little wooden ships in the harbor. She thought of the poor people of Jamtan and her promises to Alpha. Then she looked at the bubbling sea below her where she saw hundreds, no, *thousands* of these demon-fish emerging from the water, beating their wings, in pursuit. She looked beyond and below them to the unblinking eyes that would not release her. She felt herself flickering, dissolving, and breaking apart. Everything inside of her told her to flee as far and as fast as she could. So Zamar fled.

Mustering what little force she had left after a day of ghastly trials. She flew against the weight that pulled her. She flew as the sharks surrounded her. She climbed as high as she could into the sky and she flew east away from the sea as fast as she could. She did not look down, and she did not look back. She left her family, her world, and all that she knew behind her. Zamar flew furiously for hours and hours. She flew higher and faster than she ever had before until finally her airy body and her mighty will gave out. Zamar the Muslima came crashing down from the heavens at the base of the Great Pyramid of Giza.

☪

As she fled from death—and from what had been her life—what she could not see and what she did not know is that two of her children still drew breath. Whisper, Hush, Samba and Demba had indeed perished. But the two taller corpses that lay next to the door of their hut did not belong to the oldest set of twins. They did not belong to two children trying to flee from the fire, but rather to Khalifa and Mariama, Sokhna's two youngest children, who had heard the first explosions and rushed to awaken their younger siblings. When the Greek Fire hit the hut, their bodies were engulfed by flames and tar and they died almost instantly.

On this morning—as on every other morning—Tamsir and Echo had awakened simultaneously just before first light. They still slept holding hands on the same mat.

Every morning, one or the other would awaken to find their sibling staring them directly in the eye. They called it the race to the dawn. And as they walked hand-in-hand to the middle of the compound for water to make their ablutions, they tallied the score for the month. They would also talk of their dream from the night before. On most nights they had the same dream, which they each saw a little bit differently. On this particular morning, they were puzzling over why they had not dreamt at all as they dipped their small gourd into the large calabash. It was at this very moment that the first cannonballs had fallen.

They immediately rushed back toward their hut, but cannonballs and fire blocked their way. At a distance, they saw Khalifa, Mariama, and their own hut completely covered in flames. They ran through the village looking for Alpha, then Sokhna, then *anyone*. There was fire and chaos everywhere. They heard Momar calling from a distance, and they ran uphill and toward the edge of town trying to follow, but then they heard the voices of two strange men, so they hid. That was when the bullets began to fly. The children stayed hidden for hours. They saw their father shot dead by the slavers, and each reached for the other's mouth to keep them from screaming and giving away their location. But soon enough the dogs came and ferreted them out of their hiding place inside one of the village granaries.

Now the only surviving children of Al-Fahim bin Ahmad, and Zamar bint Nazreel were cowering in the hold of a slave ship. Separated for the first time in their lives, they were tied to opposite ends of the galley and attached to their classmates from the Qur'an school by the neck. They could not see each other. 589 of their friends and family members were with them. Most were packed into the horizontal barracks of the *Jezebel's* hold like cords of firewood. 396 lay broken or burned in the earth of Jamtan, including their beloved father, Alpha Ba, the Friend of God. Of the 1081 souls that had gone to their beds the night before in the most peaceful village in Futa, only 96 women, children, and elders had managed to flee to safety. Their bodies were free, but they would never escape what had happened to them and their loved ones on that day. Though much of their village was chained with them, without each other Tamsir and Echo now felt very much alone. So as the *Jezebel* sat in the harbor of Saint Louis Island, salt and fear both hung heavy in the air, and the twins knew with terrible certainty that an ocean of sorrows lay before them.

EPILOGUE

Awakening again as if from a dream, Adam took in the world around him. It was grey and lifeless compared to the vivid colors and all-encompassing vibrancy of the Garden. For the first time in some time, Hawa was not beside him. He cried out for her.

Opening her eyes to the world, Hawa too felt alone and terrified. The man and woman stumbled over dirt, rock, and mud for what felt like an eternity. Desperately calling out in the wild, they finally found one another.

This sweet embrace too seemed to last an eternity. Tears poured down their faces like rain, then rain poured over their bodies like a flood. Half-blinded by the downpour, they scrambled for shelter.

Soaked to the skin, a breeze sent shivers through them. They felt hunger in their bellies; that emptiness inside them called to be filled. They lamented the loss of the Garden.

Their bodies ached with weariness, but more than this, their hearts ached with longing. They longed to hear the Voice again, to feel Him near.

The End of Book One

ABOUT KAARONICA EVANS-WARE

Kaaronica Evans-Ware was born and raised in Decatur, Illinois. She graduated from Northwestern University with a degree in Communication. She lives in Michigan with her husband and three children. She has lived in Africa, France, and England. When she isn't traveling, she enjoys the simple pleasures of life with her beloved family.

A BRIEF AUTHOR NOTE:

The novel you just read took seven years, four months, and sixteen days to write. The inspiration for this book came after my husband, an African and Islamic History professor, returned from a research trip to Futa Toro, Senegal. There, he met a man who claimed a jinn ancestor. While it is true that this book was inspired by that one little claim, the world carefully crafted on these pages came from many hours of research and interviews and many, many more hours of prayerful reflection.